HOMAGE TO CZERNY

Originally published in German as *Schule der Geläufigkeit*, by Suhrkamp Verlag, Frankfurt, 1977; revised edition published by Residenz Verlag in 1985
Copyright © 1977, 1985, 2000 by Jung und Jung, Salzburg und Wien
Translation copyright © 2008 by Jean M. Snook

First English translation, 2008

Library of Congress Cataloging-in-Publication Data

Jonke, Gert, 1946-
[Schule der Geläufigkeit. English]
 Homage to Czerny : studies in virtuoso technique / Gert Jonke ; translation by Jean M. Snook.
  p. cm.
 ISBN 978-1-56478-501-5 (alk. paper)
 I. Snook, Jean M., 1952- II. Title.
PT2670.O5S313 2008
833'.914--dc22

2008012437

Partially funded by a grant from the Illinois Arts Council, a state agency, and by the University of Illinois at Urbana-Champaign

The author and publisher would like to thank the Austrian Federal Ministry of Education, Arts and Culture for financial assistance toward this translation

Cover art by Nicholas Motte / design by Danielle Dutton

www.dalkeyarchive.com

Printed on permanent/durable acid-free paper and bound in the United States of America

HOMAGE TO CZERNY:

STUDIES IN VIRTUOSO TECHNIQUE

BY GERT JONKE

TRANSLATED FROM THE GERMAN BY JEAN M. SNOOK

DALKEY ARCHIVE PRESS 🅂 CHAMPAIGN AND LONDON

J

What you theater people call your tradition
is nothing more than what keeps you
parasites comfortable!
—Gustav Mahler

The map here
has train tracks drawn on it
that lead into the coming autumn
into the smoke of the burned-off fields of stubble
it also shows dangerous trapdoors
through which people slip down into the root cellar

Here on the edge of the map there's just enough space for this poem
because the memory of you can never stop
and since you've been away from me my
feeling that things are as they should be has become more foreign to me
it blurts out what it wants
and I try to silence it again

I had already lost myself in you so completely
fallen in love with you that soon you
will no longer be able to find anything more
of me in you nor anywhere else

The things we dream are so systematically learned
we long for something we can't understand
that we feel safe and secure with
until it too has been made clear
because even that which remains incomprehensible
becomes trivial with time our fears
and dreams are afraid of us
they sort themselves out by running away
and playing a game of Rorschach on the terrace with a view

Then when the snow of the coming winter arrives and
completely hides the whole neighborhood together with its chairs shovels storerooms
under its blanket of snow
I will very likely do the same by painting so much white over this map here
except for the bit on the edge with the poem for
you
that it then once again in all aspects
corresponds to the details of the prevailing truth of the landscape
so that the painstakingly portrayed orientation here
is not you know too quickly lost

THE PRESENCE OF MEMORY

In the exclusive residential district on the edge of the city, the photographer Anton Diabelli and his sister Johanna lived in an elegant house with a spacious park-like garden that stretched to the nearby foothills, and, once a year, on the hottest days, the siblings had their summer garden party, to which, in addition to members of the politically-minded middle class, they invited several artists and above all many of the people variously involved in the further development of intellectual life, together with all their attendant staff, and as someone not exactly unfamiliar with the house, I had dropped by that afternoon to help if necessary with the final preparations, and in the process have a few drinks before the beginning of the festivities, so that I would seem more tolerable to myself later in those confined surroundings.

I came at just the right time to be able to help Johanna hang the oil paintings on the trees—a cycle of garden pictures done especially by the painter Florian Waldstein for this park and the summer garden parties held in it—precision work whose complexity could hardly be grasped by an outsider: the individual pictures portrayed exactly those parts of the garden that were covered by the surfaces of the respective pictures, and the portrayals were so lifelike that they were constantly being confused from every angle with the respective parts of nature itself, which is why it was absolutely necessary to take the utmost care in hanging the exhibits in their intended places to the smallest fraction of a millimeter if the works were to achieve their full effect as planned by the artist. We were just hanging a picture whose surface was to cover the view of the gate opening onto the garden, on which exactly this garden gate had been painted—when you stood in front of it you could really be tempted to leave the garden not by going around the painting in the direction of the garden gate but *by stepping into the picture, opening the door represented in the picture, disappearing behind it into the picture*—when we heard a radio playing somewhere announce that we would next hear the promising contemporary poet Kalkbrenner; then we heard Kalkbrenner give one of his popular lectures, supposedly for the common man, and this time he really took it all the way, talking about different paintings of the natural world, saying that we recognize paintings of the world because the things represented on or in them are usually things that are directly or indirectly connected with the world, and they are usually hung on the walls of the world, although in principle it's possible to put them somewhere else; however, if a picture of the world is hung on a wall of the world, and if the picture exactly represents the world in which it hangs, then it can easily happen that the world in which the attentive viewer finds himself is perhaps not a world at all but rather a picture of the world within a world or within a picture of the world, etc.

Anton Diabelli was going through the park with a Polaroid camera hung around his neck, inspecting the servants' preparations for the coming evening.

My brother is one of the most peculiar people I know, said Johanna, and sometimes I have the impression that reality becomes believable to him only when he's taken pictures of it with one of his cameras, has them lying in front of him, can let them disappear into his pockets and files and then can bring them to light again; as a result, there are many things he only experiences long after they have happened, they've simply escaped him until then. Before he can experience something, he often has to sit through many hours in his darkroom.

Diabelli was photographing nonstop in the garden and comparing the finished pictures coming out of his camera with photos that he was fishing out of his jacket pockets.

What's your brother doing? I asked.

He's comparing the photos he took of last year's party, Johanna answered, with the positions of things as they have been laid out for this evening.

Why?

So there aren't any mistakes.

What mistakes?

Everything should be exactly as it was at last year's party, answered the photographer's sister. Whispering so that I wouldn't understand, she consulted with her brother, who was passing by, after which he looked at me sternly, sizing me up; and with an expression that showed he was aware of the great responsibility weighing on him, he said in his most serious voice, as if he were entrusting me with managing the empty coffers of the City Council: If you promise not to talk with anyone about it and not to give anything away, we can tell you something important, albeit confidentially.

What's going to take place here this evening, said Johanna, is not supposed to be one of our usual summer parties, but rather

an exact reflection, no, much more than a reflection: a REPETI-
TION OF THE PARTY that we had last year on the same day at
the same time.

It's supposed to be exactly the same party again, added Diabelli.

You mean, I said, the people last year didn't quite understand
the party correctly, so you want to offer it to them again?

The same guests, said Johanna, are going to have the same conversations at the same time and tell the same stories they did last
year, with the same movements, the same gestures, same looks,
same sentiments.

You're confusing the course of our lives, I said, with the photographic paper that lets your brother copy the same picture over
and over again as often as he wants.

We haven't explained our intentions to anyone, said the photographer, so we aren't influencing the normal course of events.

I don't know if this is going to work, said Johanna, but it's worth
a try.

We have to see if it's possible to establish a congruity of chronologically sequential feelings, sensations, thoughts, relationships,
inferences, and insights, explained Diabelli—possibly not just
congruity, but identity. Don't you see what we're after? Whether
people can still feel, sense, think, experience, and discover exactly
the same things one year later.

You're trying to change memories back into the present moment, I said, but the laws of nature won't allow that.

The laws of nature, Johanna replied, are you really talking about
the laws of nature? Isn't it a law of nature that not only has next
to nothing changed in the past year, but in fact that everything has
remained just the same, and is exactly as unbearable, unjust, and
miserable now as then? And isn't it a law of nature that we've man-

aged to preserve all the monotony surrounding us and the prevailing untenable relationships so well that our attempted *repetition of the party* ought to be child's play?

What do you hope to achieve with this? I asked.

My brother, replied Johanna, has an admittedly and completely lunatic and academic interest in whether the guests—none of whom can have any idea of how we've prepared things—will unknowingly and, as it were, somehow *correctly* slip and slide into exactly the same *enactment* of their feelings, relationships, thoughts, and insights as they did a year ago. For my part, said Johanna, I'm above all curious as to whether these people are really as unimaginative and lifeless as they seem, in which case they will once again happily and contentedly amuse themselves with the same nonsense that dominated the party last year, without noticing what's going on in the slightest.

And that's just the sort of mindlessness I don't want to be involved in, I replied, especially not so knowingly and helplessly.

I said: I would rather not be present.

On the radio we heard the announcer say we had just heard a repeat broadcast of a lecture by Kalkbrenner, and immediately after that came the weather report: It was going to rain in the night.

Did you hear that, I said, it's going to rain tonight, that's the beginning already.

Quite right, said Diabelli, that really is how it begins, because last year there was also rain forecast for the night of the party, but then the storm changed course on the way here or got stuck somewhere else, but in any case, as you'll remember, we had a clear night and could see the stars in the sky.

I turned away, wanting to leave silently, without further dispute.

It wasn't so much Diabelli's stubborn insistence on being right that alienated me as it was Johanna's smugness; and when she spoke of the circumstances of our lives, she always hinted at a still prevalent but next to unrecognizable form of suppression, consisting of all of us repeatedly being *used* to our disadvantage— primarily to demonstrate to several other people, at our expense, that the reassuring feeling they have that all the things they do behind our backs are an indispensable precondition for our continued existence is entirely justified—and yet, while she said that sort of thing, she believed herself to be free of the stereotypes of this kind of existence, in which she herself would use others, pointing out their dependence, especially when it was a matter of their dependence on her, to confirm her own independence, to which she unconditionally *subordinated* the events of her private life—for example, the coming party.

She felt most free when she could suspect someone of wanting to suppress her, she exerted the greatest pressure when she could excuse herself by saying she had been suppressed, and even when she was able to reciprocate the dreamy desire someone felt for her with a close affection, she interpreted that person's desire to be with her as an attack on her independence.

I had already left through the park gate onto the country road, paying no attention to Diabelli calling after me, first asking me to come back right away, then demanding that I do so, saying that I couldn't let him down right now and that I was urgently needed, and then I heard him reproach his sister: You shouldn't have told that composer anything, this is a serious abuse of the trust we placed in him!

The sky is like a streaked convex lens hovering over the plain, I thought, focusing the afternoon light over the city, and soon the huts and shrubs at the edge of the dry forest would begin to smoke, and already I saw a haze rising from the suburban fields when I heard steps behind me—Johanna had followed me, caught up to me, held on to me, was clasping her hands behind my head, looking at me, and saying:

Don't you remember, my love, how we two were together last year after the party? And wouldn't you like to see if we can come together again tomorrow exactly the same way, experiencing each other again so intensely, so beautifully again though as never before, and also perhaps to see how the limitations of time can fall away forever, and not only from our relationship, so that secure in this knowledge we can then always receive each other in our own unique ways? Wouldn't that be reason enough to stay here now?

The preparations for the evening festivities were finished, and I was standing with Diabelli in the farthest third of the park, at the edge of the bank of a small pond covered with algae and full of foul-smelling water, looking at a moss-covered sandstone statue set up there, presumably of some ancient nymph, Diabelli was doing the talking, continuing to offer me logical supporting arguments for repeating the party, going on about it being the same date on the same weekday, separated only by a single year, a co-incidence that could occur only once in thousands of years, but that was entirely self-explanatory due to the systematically logical necessity of inserting leap-days from time to time to keep the calendar accurate.

Call it off, I said, you have to call everything off, we can't afford to have a repetition of all the worst possible accidents that happened last year but that no one knew about and that you can't be expecting.

Instead of answering me he pulled out a photo, here, he said, a photo of you at last year's party that you probably haven't seen.

In the photo I was standing beside the sandstone statue, looking at the grass with an uncertain, searching expression. I looked at the statue, then at the photo of myself beside the statue, something bothered me, wasn't right—ah, it was the statue's head, in the photo of last year's party the statue's head was missing, whereas the statue in front of me definitely had a head.

I handed the photo back to Diabelli, asking if he didn't notice anything about it.

No, he didn't notice anything peculiar about the photo. Look, I said, from this point on, the repetition of the party can't take place, as is evident from this picture, because in the photo from last year's party the statue, as you can see, is missing its head, but if you look at the statue actually standing here right now, it does indeed have a head, that can hardly be contested, so the statue that's standing here in front of us, I explained to the photographer, can't possibly be the same statue that was standing here at last year's party, which, as the photo demonstrates, did not have a head, so it must have been an entirely different statue, and this detail alone, that he, Diabelli, had not taken into consideration, was enough to cause the whole repetition party to fail before it had even properly begun.

Diabelli wasn't very impressed by my reasoning, hardly took any notice of it, he doesn't understand it, I thought, it's probably coming too fast for him, presumably he doesn't want to admit to any of it, and his indifference or arrogance in dealing with my explanation of the completely new conceptual situation affecting the coming evening caused me to repeat my argument for him, making it a little more graphic, a little more tangible, so I took the photo again, asking him to look at it a little more closely, here, I said, you see that the statue in the photo is actually headless, I pointed with my finger at the spot where the statue stopped, at the break in its neck, where its head must have broken off, do you see that, I asked the photographer, who nodded in the affirmative, then I pointed at the statue in front of us, and here you see the statue, but this statue very definitely has a head, as you must be able to see, I stepped closer to the statue in order to draw Diabelli's attention to the irrefutable head atop the statue's neck, possibly, I had been thinking, he doesn't see the head, he doesn't want to see it, and for that reason I wanted to draw his attention to it quite forcefully, otherwise I thought he would deny that the statue had a head, look, here's the head on the statue, I called to Diabelli, and yet here in the photo from last year, I repeated my explanation, there's no head, nothing there, right on this spot, with my right index finger I traced the line on the statue's neck where at last year's party the head had been broken off, somehow there at that spot the head of the statue from last year's party had broken off, fallen down, I demonstrated all this to Diabelli as graphically as possible, and look, I said then, the head on this statue set up here is firmly attached, very firmly, it won't break off from the neck as easily as must have happened with the statue in the photo, and in order to prove to the photographer how firmly the head on the statue in front of us was attached to its base, I went over to grab hold of the sandstone nymph by her neck, but I had hardly touched the back of her head, very lightly, when it suddenly broke away from the stone goddess's neck, falling at my feet in the grass.

Diabelli took a picture in that very instant, he pulled the photo from his camera, here, look, he said, and I saw myself standing beside the sandstone statue, looking at the grass with an uncertain, searching expression: it was an identical photo to the photo from the previous year that he had just been showing me, and when we compared the two pictures one to the other, we couldn't find a single detail that would let us differentiate them.

Diabelli picked up the statue's fallen head from the grass and put it back on the nymph. This sort of thing is never as firmly attached as you think, he said.

I looked at some of the other Diabelli photos from the previous year, in one of them I could see many of the guests standing around the little pond in the back of the garden, their eyes fixed gravely on the water, and then I remembered music like I'd never heard before and haven't heard since—to think I had forgotten it!—the most beautiful combination of tones I ever heard. I know what you're intending to do, I said to Diabelli. You want to transform memory into the present moment again and to freeze all the future hours of our lives so that you can combine the pictures of our one-year-old past into a single monumental photograph, and in order to produce this photograph, you want to avail yourself of part of our approaching present, *but I remember music that until then I would not have thought possible, and which to this day unfortunately I have not heard again. Everything got resolved in those tones. That piece of music, I explained to Diabelli, which unfortunately was very short, interrupted the party last year, if only for a brief moment, and afterwards, because no one could explain it, was forgotten or denied as soon as the sounds had died away. Naturally, such music unfortunately is not repeatable. However, if contrary to my expectations that sort of thing could be experienced again, then I can only hope that the music will interrupt tonight's party for a longer time than last year, so that it can't be as easily forgotten or denied.*

I remember *how it took me by surprise, the start of the party,* suddenly a group of people had pushed their way in through the garden gate and spread out between the bushes in the park, dusk was already falling, the party music had begun to play, Chinese lanterns were lit, unfamiliar faces gleamed at each other, the people wandered past the pictures hanging from the trees, pausing to look at them hesitantly, standing closer and closer to them, as if they were stepping into them or getting sucked in, being used as figurative, moveable, representative figures in Florian Waldstein's exhibit, Florian Waldstein who was sitting silently in a wicker chair, and whenever anyone said a word to him, he wrinkled his brow, turned his eyes away, and made such a pained impression with his gestures that it was understood he was asking most politely to be left alone.

If you were more closely acquainted with him, you wouldn't misread these expressions, which outsiders interpreted as arrogance—especially not once you understood how to figure out when he wanted to be spoken to and when not, because his flamboyant show of annoyance could just as well cause him *not* to be spoken to when he actually wanted to be as it could warn people away when he didn't.

In no case may he be spoken to, I heard Johanna explaining to the proctologist's wife, when he is in the process of observing something—a landscape, a building, people—as he is now. The worst thing you can do to our painter is to comment to him about something he is just then in the process of observing—he regards it as outrageously presumptuous of people to impose their own will on his observations with their intrusive remarks.

Helping Johanna explain the painter's manners, I said, you're only allowed to talk to him when he has his eyes shut, then you can to some extent be sure that you aren't disturbing any of his observations. If he isn't observing anything and thus expects to be spoken to, and if you're a close friend of his, he'll conduct *a conversation with his eyes closed*. Those are the most interesting conversations you can have with him, the sight of his closed eyes lends his refined manner of speech an additional sense of great calm, deliberateness, and wisdom.

I can see that, replied the proctologist's wife.

In no case should you make the mistake, Johanna emphasized, of speaking to him right away if you should feel yourself being observed by him, even if it does appear initially as if he were waiting for you to say something—because if he's looking at you, that's always first and foremost a sure sign that he's observing you, and in no case should you interrupt him in these observations of your person, yes, that would be the biggest mistake you could make.

Only when he has his eyes closed, you have to remember that.

And even then it's advantageous to find out beforehand whether he has his eyes shut because he isn't observing anything or whether he has his eyes shut because he's sleeping.

Because when the painter has his eyes shut because he's sleeping, he's involved in the most complicated observations imaginable.

Because when he sleeps, he's observing his dreams.

Look who's over there, said Johanna, our hospital architect. He has made his mark by both planning and building all the insane asylums of our city.

He's not only an outstanding admirer of art, but also regards himself as an artist, and in that respect he has accomplished at least one great thing: No artist who suddenly goes crazy needs to pay anything for a temporary or even a permanent stay in one of the insane asylums that the hospital architect planned and built, which he regards as his own works of art. It's the most natural thing in the world, the hospital architect keeps explaining, that an artist should have no financial problems while himself residing in or disappearing into a work of art, as the architect describes his insane asylums.

At a furious tempo the poet Kalkbrenner came steaming in through the garden gate in a euphoric mood, pushing his way panting through the packed group of partygoers and making straight for me, I saw he seemed to have gotten even fatter since the last time we'd met and looked now as if he would burst, his greeting was very friendly, at last we get to see each other again. In his present state he had to take care not to be unnecessarily squeezed by anyone, he said, or he'd jump out of his skin.

He drew me to a table in the salon and called out to the servant who was hurrying past: Waiter, please bring me two bottles of beer and a champagne bucket right away!

He absolutely had to cheer me up, the poet explained animatedly, pulling out a stopwatch, pay attention, he said, here, look, the stopwatch, he promised me the demonstration of a unique phenomenon would follow immediately. The champagne bucket and the two beers were already standing on the table, so watch, he said, and took the first bottle of beer and poured it out, aiming the open bottleneck into the champagne bucket and starting the stopwatch at the exact point in time when the beer began to stream from the bottle into the bucket, of course the bottle was empty almost immediately, and then Kalkbrenner halted the timer. You do look astonished, he said, here, and held the face of the stopwatch up to my eyes, look, exactly seven seconds, and that's a measurement of the shortest possible time it takes for a full bottle of beer to flow freely out under favorable, natural conditions. And now pay close attention, he said, taking the second full beer bottle and holding it up to his mouth, starting the stopwatch again at exactly the point in time when the beer began to cross his lips, it streamed rapidly out of the bottleneck into Kalkbrenner's neck, the empty bottle gurgled, and of course the poet had pressed the stopwatch again at the proper time, when the last bit of beer had crossed his oral cavity, and held the face of the stopwatch toward me to have a look, now you'll be amazed, he said, here, five seconds, two seconds faster than when it flowed freely out of the bottle, what do you say about that, how can you explain it? Of course I didn't have an answer, Kalkbrenner gave a satisfied laugh, yes, and many others had already been amazed by this trick. Why, Kalkbrenner asked, does the same volume of beer out of the same bottle flow at a considerably higher speed through my neck into my stomach than it flows freely through the air under considerably more favorable conditions—whether into a champagne bucket or somewhere else, it makes no difference, and even if Kalkbrenner had poured the first bottle not into the champagne bucket, which he had done primarily for reasons of cleanliness, but simply onto the parquet floor, the indisputable rate of seven seconds would have remained the same. Although according to the laws of logic it should be the other way around, because the beer would have to lose considerable time en route to the stomach, not only because of the relative narrowness of the human neck, but also because of the friction along the inner wall of the esophagus, not to mention that the impediment of having to swallow while drinking would not only slow the beer's flow even more, but also occasionally interrupt it, Kalkbrenner explained, so, therefore, if the beer takes seven seconds to flow freely out of the bottle through the air when the bottle is held at an angle of, say, sixty or seventy degrees, to aid the rate of flow, then for its passage through the neck to the stomach, if we take into account the frictional resistance to the liquid along the inner wall of the esophagus, we should add on at least three seconds, which means that in the best case scenario the beer would need at least ten seconds!

So why do I need only half the time, namely five seconds? asked

Kalkbrenner. Waiter, another two bottles of beer please, he called to the servant passing by.

His ability to suppress all his swallowing reflexes while drinking would be hard to imitate, yet I was supposed to give it a try.

I attempted to drink without swallowing and choked violently, which gave Kalkbrenner occasion to recite two of his latest alexandrines:

When coping with some aspect of ourselves is hard,
We choke it down, and eat ourselves along with it!

Some of the guests had gathered around to observe this demonstration of the Kalkbrenner phenomenon.

Look over there, said Johanna, let me introduce you to the proctologist.

Of course you don't know what a proctologist is, said Kalkbrenner, not many people do; a proctologist is a physician who deals exclusively with the human asshole, he has specialized in it, although I personally am of the opinion that these assholes have specialized in him: This doctor occupies himself all day long with the hind ends of our city's people, examining those parts in the most scientific manner, and because he mistakenly believes that he can best recover from the asses of the world in the company of so-called highly intellectual, highly artistic people, because he thinks that art is the opposite of the human ass, he doesn't miss any of these parties; what can possibly be going on in the mind of a person who is continually occupied his whole life long with the assholes that are multiplying and reproducing around him at an increasingly alarming rate? Mind you, he chose his profession himself. Well, said Johanna, it hasn't occurred to him yet to complain about his unusual existence, mainly because all the people out there who are condemned to have the same rear end their entire lives are obviously prepared to pay him very well to give them the impression that he's seeing a completely unique backside each time, isn't that right, Doctor?

The fact that I drink without swallowing explains next to nothing, said Kalkbrenner, who continued to explain this phenomenon because we still had no idea how the small diameter of the outlet pipe or the naturally occurring frictional opposition presented by the wall of the esophagus were overcome so quickly, and of course we still needed the answer to the main question: how is a drainage rate achieved through the throat that is not only equal to the regular speed under more favorable conditions, but is actually considerably accelerated, so that a record of only five seconds is set instead of seven—two seconds faster than that of beer flowing freely out of the bottle?

The servant brought several bottles of beer, and Kalkbrenner repeated his demonstration with the same result when we compared the times.

It's a matter, whispered Kalkbrenner, who was finally telling us his secret, of certain motions that have to be carried out by certain muscles and clusters of cartilage here in the throat, you see, *to suck in* the flowing beer with the esophagus, get it? The beer has to be *sucked* down into the stomach by the esophagus if such acceleration is to be achieved; you have to picture your esophagus as a suction pipe.

He compared his entire food intake and digestion apparatus to a vacuum cleaner—he seemed to find the words "vacuum cleaner" suitable as a new form of address for people, in fact, going on to refer to human beings as biological sucking apparatuses that suck up their unpalatable environment, suck it up, suck it down, suck it in, and when they have sucked themselves full, they burst and spray apart if they can't manage to blow out the sucked-in, sucked-up stuff again somewhere else; the blower really has to work properly, he said, that's the most important thing.

I heard the hospital architect explaining to someone that as an amateur musician the proctologist is such an excellent trumpet player that he once stood in at short notice for the first trumpet of our city's philharmonic orchestra who had fallen ill and played the solo part in Alexander Scriabin's *Poème de l'extase.*

Of course I'll have to keep working on it, said Kalkbrenner, to get even faster, my next goal is four seconds, then three, etc., so that some day I'll be just like a runner who's already at the finish line when the starting gun goes off, with no measurable loss of time, or, he said, you throw a discus, and the discus glides through the clouds out into the universe, never to return, so there's no need to measure the distance it's traveled, because its flight won't come to an end in your lifetime.

And over there in the corner, said Johanna, is the undertaker, also a great admirer of art.

An exemplary reader of our literature, Kalkbrenner added, who's outrageously adept at carrying off everything we produce, a patron who never lets go until he's laid to rest all he can get his hands on, until the works of art he's devoured have rotted away inside him, making room for him to bury new works of art, which, thanks to his position and the success of his funeral home, is a negligible expense at best.

Mr. Schwarzkopf, Johanna asked the funeral director, we know you're always making sure that all the known and unknown sculptors of our city get the most lucrative contracts for gravestones and monuments, but is it true, as I've heard recently, that you've purchased a large piece of land in the center of our biggest cemetery because you finally want to realize one of your oldest dreams, namely, to erect a so-called "Monument to the Unknown Artist" on that spot? Yes, replied the funeral director, quite right, and I intend to have this "Monument to the Unknown Artist" made by a sculptor who is not only completely unknown to everyone else, but even to myself.

When an artist is buried, said Johanna, it is to Funeral Director Schwarzkopf's credit that he never presents his surviving family members with a bill.

The master of funerals nodded in agreement.

Which means that each and every artist, Johanna said, is guaranteed a first-class burial in our city at no charge.

All our sculptors, said Kalkbrenner, who incidentally even without the existence of this gentleman here wouldn't be in a position to do much more than work on different types of gravestones in our city to earn their keep, would soon be in a state of financial ruin without all the business he refers to them, but thanks to his zealous assistance they have worked their way up to become the richest and most prosperous among all their artist colleagues. Schwarzkopf, too, is one of those people who think that the company of artists, of all people, will bring him peace and quiet from his increasingly confusing and unmanageable funeral business, which is why he seeks out such parties like this when he doesn't happen to have to bury something.

Listen, said Kalkbrenner, if you need money urgently sometime, then the best thing you can do is to turn to this gentleman here who has his diploma in the funeral and burial business, you can always get an advance from him if you're willing to sign a contract agreeing to compose the funeral music for your own first-class funeral, isn't that right, Mr. Schwarzkopf? Of course, agreed Schwarzkopf, if you want you can sign today and I'll pay you the advance right away.

He placed a preprinted contract in front of me, which I signed immediately, if somewhat hesitantly, because I was really short of cash, and so I thereby undertook from that time forth to make no further efforts to become an immortal artist, but rather to leave all matters pertaining to my burial to the co-signatory funeral home which would, however, leave me completely free to write my own burial music, which would have its première performance at my funeral and would never again be played by anyone, because the score would be destroyed after the burial, primarily for reasons of piety.

Congratulations, said Schwarzkopf in a loud voice, and Kalkbrenner congratulated me too and said that in order to do justice to such a ceremonial occasion, he would put on a "simultaneous demonstration," especially for me, then gave me the stopwatch and asked me to note the time, just the time he held the bottle to his lips, because the time it takes for the beer to run out freely is, he said, as you know, an immutable constant, whereas the time taken to suck the beer into his stomach was variable and could get better or worse. He had already put one bottle to his lips with his left hand while he tipped the other bottle with his right and let it run out freely; concentrating hard, I watched the sucking, funnel-shaped Kalkbrenner head with its neck winding down like a corkscrew into his thorax, I pressed the knob on the stopwatch, and already the bottle held to his mouth was empty, while the other, free-running one, kept splashing for at least three more seconds. Four seconds, a new record, cheered Kalkbrenner, the first time ever! The crowd was enthusiastic and gave him thunderous applause, only the proctologist was of a different opinion,

GOETHE had been able to do much better than that, and in this regard Kalkbrenner was just a puny epigone.

Waiter, please bring us a dry champagne now, Kalkbrenner called to the servant.

You pig, the latter replied, what do you think you're doing, pouring out a whole bottle of beer onto the parquet like that?

I only now noticed that Kalkbrenner, in all the excitement of his successful breaking of a new record, had forgotten to hold the free-flowing bottle over the champagne bucket, so the beer had poured onto the spotless parquet floor—Kalkbrenner apologized to the servant, but added that every conventional cleaning product contained a considerably higher percentage of alcohol than a bottle of beer, so he didn't understand what all the fuss was about.

Several ladies and gentlemen who held high positions in the city administration had seated themselves on a corner of the terrace where there was a good view of the city lights at night, of course they were always busy thinking and talking about the many and diverse problems of the municipality and, relaxed by the festive mood of the evening, they were exchanging their opinions on these matters much more freely than usual and in an informal manner.

The lady who was the city manager asked the gentleman who had been introduced to me as the building inspector: Do you have any idea, Mr. Jagusch, why the northern part of the city that we see over there against the sky has always such a magnificent red glow in the early evening hours?

Well, that's perfectly clear, replied the building inspector, it's because in the north side nothing is clear—that is, everything's covered by a blanket of smoke from the factories there; have you ever been in the north side of the city, City Manager?

No, she answered, she hadn't been there yet, and she mentioned her very tight schedule.

Good for you, said Mr. Jagusch the building inspector, save yourself the trouble.

I just wanted to know, said the city manager, why the part of town that we see at the horizon always has such a magnificent red glow in the evening, what is your opinion on this, Town Planner?

No, no, replied the old man she had addressed as the town planner, I'm not saying anything else, I've already said everything.

There are several theories, said the city gardener, a man by the name of Jacksch: perhaps the most plausible is that the rays of the setting sun get caught in the smoke and can't get through, so that the glow of sunset is conserved for a few hours by the smoke that the north side of town was built with and only disperses later in the night.

Did you just say that the north side of the city is made of smoke? enquired the city manager.

Quite right, replied Jacksch, my sources tell me that the building material used in constructing it was smoke.

What nonsense, interjected Jagusch, who has ever heard of such a thing, would you explain to me please how you could build even a single house out of smoke, let alone an entire part of our city! A house made of smoke, don't make me laugh!

I have it on good authority that this is indeed the case, replied Jacksch, or can you prove to me that it isn't? When was the last time you were there, Mr. Jagusch—tell me, when?

Of course I've never gone there myself, answered the building inspector, why would I, but the employees responsible for that region, who are my subordinates and report to me daily, know very well how to distinguish between solid concrete and smoke.

It's probably smoke concrete or smoke brick, said Jacksch.

No, no, answered Jagusch, it isn't smoky there because the smoke was used as a building material, it's made by all the factories that operate there and so has permanently shrouded that entire part of the city.

An especially important and effective protective measure for that part of the city, I imagine, said the city manager, to protect our factories from the corrosive effects of the weather.

No, that's not it either, replied the building inspector; quite the contrary, the smoke was meant to be blown away by the wind as soon as it left the factories and to be carried off by clouds; but it turns out that the wind is too high up, you know.

So why didn't they build smokestacks up into the wind, to the clouds?

They did, they did all that, but the smokestacks were still much too low, on the north side of the city the wind and the clouds move much higher up in the sky than the smokestacks reached, so that the smoke was constantly forced down from the tops of the smokestacks by the atmospheric calm that is typical of that part of the city, and so now the smoke envelops the entire north side, day and night, do you understand?

So why didn't they plan and build the smokestacks higher, so that their tips reached the wind and the clouds?

I can give you a definitive answer to that, replied Jagusch. When the architects back then planned these factories that are so indispensable to our city and the proper functioning of our economy, planned them together with their smokestacks, I can't remember how many, around a hundred I think, the specialists' calculations for their optimum height turned out to be much too low, because during the project studies on site, the north side of the city had been experiencing a tremendously strong wind, which was remarkable in that it was so unusual there, in every respect absolutely atypical for the north side, because as you know even when a real storm blows through our city and the surrounding region, it nevertheless always remains completely calm on the north side, and only there, the wind simply will not blow through there, it's always refused to blow through the north side of the city, it always avoids it, circumvents it, blows right around it, but back then, of all times, when the architects were planning the factories for the north side of the city, it was extremely windy in the north, no, not just windy, but downright stormy, although at the same time it was completely calm everywhere else in city and also in the surrounding countryside, but right then and exclusively in the north side of the city it was storming for the first time, as it never had before or since, and that was of course a real stroke of bad luck, as you can imagine, because that was just when the architects responsible for the construction of the northern part of our city were carrying out their surveys and drawing conclusions about the necessary height of the smokestacks from the strong storms prevailing during their visit, which conclusions would have been absolutely correct if the wind that was blowing then in the north part of the city had continued to blow thereafter, but which unfortunately proved to be false immediately after the factories went into operation, but of course the architects couldn't be blamed for the fact that their wind had stopped blowing; the height of a smokestack is calculated according to the average weather conditions at the time of the calculations, the higher up the wind, the taller the smokestack has to be, and we should really think highly of the architects for having planned to give us any smokestacks at all for our factories during a continuous storm of that nature with the wind whistling past their ears the whole time they were doing their complicated work, since—even if the smokestacks are admittedly too short— it's a wonder they were farsighted enough to plan for so much as a single stack, and so we are highly indebted to those people for each and every smokestack that they gave us, even if they are too short! Indeed we are!

Couldn't the smokestacks have been elevated afterwards? someone asked.

Of course they could have, answered the building inspector, and they were, and with the passage of time the smokestacks have been gradually raised, always step by step, you know, higher into the sky.

Why step by step? someone asked.

There was a new problem, answered Jagusch, we were confronted with a completely new problem: The higher we extended the red brick pipes into the sky, the higher the wind and the clouds too climbed over the north side of the city, naturally without taking along even a single puff of the north side smoke, and as the movement of the atmosphere could be most precisely measured, it was proven, statistically, again and again: whenever we raised the smokestacks by so much as a single meter, the wind and the clouds too climbed one meter higher in the sky over the north part of the city, but we continued, now we raised our smokestacks, drilling into the ether, by another meter, and hardly was that done before we determined that the clouds and winds had likewise risen by one meter, exactly as though they were avoiding being touched by the tips of the smokestacks, but there still wasn't any reason to lose our nerve, now we decided to use an entirely new tactic, to use a little cunning to finally achieve the goal we had pursued for so long, and so we began work on yet another extension of the smokestacks, at first acting as though we wanted to carry out another and identical advance of our smokestacks out towards the universe—adding another meter—and no one had any reason to doubt this, most people were naturally of the opinion that this would be how we would proceed, but a small number of the initiated knew that this time the slender smokestack cylinders were going to drill up *one and a half* meters more; soon the work was finished, but immediately afterwards we determined that the wind and the clouds had also raised themselves up by exactly *one and a half* meters—no, they hadn't let themselves be fooled; well, and as you can imagine, we still didn't give up, but continued to try one plan after another for decades to come, but it was all to no avail, wasn't it, Town Planner?

No, replied the town planner, I'm not saying anything else, I've already said everything, now it's up to you to say what has to be said! Kindly keep talking!

Until one day, Jagusch said, the north city smokestacks had reached such a height that their tips would have broken through—or, how do you say, pierced, I mean, penetrated—even the thickest cloud canopy in every other district of the city, on a cloudy day, but there was no question of that happening on the north side of the city, and, well, one day they just fell over, collapsed, or they broke off, whichever, and the reason why was that we had neglected to make them proportionally thicker at the same time as we were making them higher, and so the smokestacks had remained far too thin in proportion to the fantastic height that they had one day attained, quite contrary to the original plan, you see, they shouldn't have just become higher and higher, but also wider and wider, if we wanted them to stay standing, anyway. That's why even today on the north we have this huge gray cloud of smoke fixed on the horizon like a leech hanging from the bottom of the sky, and the apartments there are the cheapest in the city.

What you're saying is all well and good, said the lady who was the city manager, but I just wanted to know why this ball of smoke hanging from or hovering in the sky—how did you put it?

Hanging from, I said, answered Jagusch.

This ball of smoke hanging from the sky in the north city, said the city manager, why does it always glow so impressively and brightly red for a while in the evenings.

I already explained that to you, said Jacksch, part of the evening light is conserved there during sunset and glows into the night for a few hours.

What nonsense, replied Jagusch: as far as he knew the cloud of smoke was artificially illuminated in the evening, an attraction to promote foreign tourism.

All of them now looked silently and thoughtfully at the northern part of the horizon where the big red Chinese lantern was hovering—or was it a balloon that could burst at any moment?

Well, what do you think, Town Planner, said the city manager, is it going to burst soon?

No, answered the old town planner, I'm not saying anything else, I've already said often enough that I've already said everything, no one can fool me about this city anymore, I've written this city off long ago, by the way did you know that a city had already been founded here before the ancient Illyrians, by a people about whom nothing else is known besides that they either left this city again soon after founding it or that they perished here? But don't go thinking that these people were driven out by the ancient Illyrians, no, because it's been historically verified that the ancient Illyrians, when they settled in this region, found the old city, or rather the remains of the old city abandoned! You'll find all this confirmed in the books published by the City Museum Press.

At the next opportunity, you know, you should really take a walk around the outside of the city, then you'll be able to see the remains of the buildings that were on stilts, the stumps of the buildings on stilts in the unbelievable number of marshes, ponds, and lakes that surround our city. It's astounding that these stumps of buildings on stilts have remained perfectly preserved to the present day, they're not rotting in the least. The people back then must have stained the wood in some secret way, these days you can't expect such careful precision work from people anymore. If you want, you can see a completely reconstructed model village of stilt-buildings in our City Museum—in the marshes around the city they've even found human cadavers that are thousands of years old and completely intact.

These bodies have been perfectly preserved by the marshy soil, you really have to go to the City Museum, several of these ancient cadavers are displayed there in glass showcases. In the bog, where people have been cutting peat for as long as anyone can remember, workers are always finding these corpses.

Even today, interjected City Gardener Jacksch, people are still getting swallowed up by the bog with alarming regularity, often monthly and sometimes even weekly. Many people go for a walk without believing that there's any danger and then get found later by the peat cutters while they're cutting peat. He had heard, said Jacksch, that in most cases the faces of these cadavers were no longer recognizable, and thus it was impossible to differentiate between a cadaver that had sunk into the marsh thousands of years ago and a completely preserved human body that had just sunk into the marsh several years, months, or weeks ago, so that we have to assume that there aren't only bodies that are thousands of years old being shown to visitors at the City Museum, but also bodies that are just a few years old, if that, and so it's our very special good fortune, said Jacksch, that one of my or your acquaintances or relatives who we haven't heard from in a while may suddenly turn up as an archaeological find in the Museum.

Even the ancient Illyrians abandoned this city soon after settling here, continued the town planner, and even the ancient Romans who came after the ancient Illyrians were forced to abandon this city or were destroyed by it in time—just think, even the ancient Romans, who weren't so easily overcome, and then the Bayuwaren, Avars, etc., who came after them, Charlemagne's troops and the hordes of Turks and Huns, they all could count their days in this city on their fingers, and that's the way it happened again and again throughout history. The town planner said, it's a joke that this city even exists, a particularly bad joke. And he knew one thing for sure: It wasn't just the ancient people who lived in buildings on stilts, no, the Illyrians, Romans, and all the other riffraff who were forced to leave this city or were destroyed by it, even in recent times more and more people have been forced to leave the city, or else have been destroyed by it.

I definitely understand your concern, I heard the building inspector say, and all of you here will certainly still remember those strange occurrences caused by natural phenomena several years ago, when water suddenly rose up out of the ground everywhere, seeping up from the bowels of the earth, even though it hadn't rained for weeks, the air was completely dry, it was one of the hottest summers I can remember, and yet the earth everywhere was slightly putrid, soaked through and through, you know, a sort of gleaming film of moisture had formed on the ground, like a transparent skin stretched tightly across the entire landscape.

Yes, I heard the editor confirm, it was a difficult wonderful time back then. I was in the stadium that afternoon for an eagerly anticipated soccer game, naturally the place was completely sold out, I went into the reporter's booth up in the top row to report on the game via radio, the two teams came running onto the field, the referee blew the whistle to start the game, initially an evenly matched game except for the usual slight superiority of the foreigners' team, which however should have been fully compensated for by our hometown advantage, until—and it had been forecast—it suddenly began to rain, and the tight strings of water drawn down from the clouds to the playing field were strung closer and closer together until I could only see the players and their movements on the field as shadowy bowling pins getting darker and lighter as they moved closer or farther away, darting unsystematically around, so that, in a word, any chance at following the game had been lost, and then to make it even worse a thick blanket of fog settled down right on the field, a single solitary cumulous cloud came floating down and covered the entire field, so I had no choice but to temporarily discontinue my broadcast.

What nonsense, Jagusch contradicted him, there wasn't the slightest trace of clouds or rain in the heat of that summer, and that's exactly what frightened and alarmed us, the fact that even heat like that couldn't keep the moisture under control, the water that was rising up from the bowels of the earth, the water kept coming, began to rot away the walls of the city, rising up through them via capillary action, mold began to grow on the mortar everywhere that not only loosened the bricks but also spread an unbearable stench, as I'm sure you'll remember.

No, no, City Gardener Jacksch contradicted him, shaking his head, it was nothing like that, you couldn't say it was a hot or dry summer at all and certainly not that the ground was moist, don't you remember anything anymore, it rained nonstop, day and night, yet the ground was completely dried out, the earth just wasn't capable of soaking up a single drop of water, instead the water just trickled away, and in the middle of the rain, just imagine, under that continual rain our gardens withered and dried up, the cornfields, *the entire harvest actually withered in the torrential rains* and died of thirst, just picture it!

Yes, just picture it, said the editor, the cloud had finally separated itself from the playing field again, floating slowly up, and it had stopped raining, the view of the playing field below was quite clear again, but now the players weren't there anymore, they were simply gone, at first people thought they had gone into the locker room temporarily, of course people tried to whistle them back out, but they were nowhere to be seen, maybe they just snuck away under cover of the cloud, the spectators went wild, they could hardly be restrained from storming the field.

What nonsense, Jagusch turned to face Jacksch, it was hot and dry like never before, but as I've already said, the ground was sopping, the mold growing on the walls gave off a terrible stench, and the only reason it didn't rise up and get everywhere was because of its weight, that was pretty lucky, that the stench only covered the ground, rolling through the streets, you only noticed it if you bent down to tie your shoelaces, a vile smell, because of which we naturally had to carry small children on our shoulders, of course nothing could be done to help our pets, at night the noise they were making got more and more unbearable, I would hardly have been able to sleep a wink without earplugs then, with the dogs howling, the cats screaming, the chickens cackling, and to make matters worse that oppressive, sultry heat . . .

It got colder and colder that summer, Jacksch replied, the rain heavier and heavier, and nevertheless the ground got drier and drier, soon it'll start to snow, I thought . . .

Isn't it unbelievable, Jagusch replied excitedly, to distort proven facts like that? Please say something, Town Planner! Make a definitive statement!

There's nothing at all to say, said the town planner, the gentlemen are both right, I'm not saying anything else, how often do I still have to say that I've already said everything, the gentlemen are both right: whereas the city gardener said it rained continually, yet the ground was so dried out that in the rain the crops withered and died, because the ground wouldn't absorb the rain water, but let it seep through instead, the building inspector said the air was hot and dry in a way we were no longer accustomed to, in spite of the alarmingly moist ground, from which water rose up and could not be kept in check even by the prevailing heat and dryness previously mentioned. The situation is quite clear, gentlemen, you're both right, it's just that you were on two different, opposite, even antipodean parts of the planet at the time, and the continual rain the city gardener mentioned, well, it simply seeped down through the ground and became the water the building inspector was referring to, the water that rose up from the ground there on the opposite part of the planet, that's perfectly clear, there's nothing at all to say about it.

I saw the old town planner indicating a large circle on the table in front of him with his finger.

Look, he said, here, the planet,

then he indicated a point on the outlined circle, and here, you see, Mr. Jacksch's rain seeping through!

Then he pointed to the opposite point on the circle, and here, he said, you see, it must have risen up, come up here again, after it had trickled through the planet, I mean the water, because it had to come out again somewhere!

And back then the city gardener was at this point on the planet, weren't you here then, Mr. Jacksch, please think carefully!

The city gardener nodded.

See, you were actually here then, I knew it, that's plausible, isn't it? Weren't you here then, Mr. Jagusch, give it your most exact consideration!

The building inspector nodded.

See, said the town planner, I knew it, you were actually here then! But you look astonished, City Manager, what do you have to say about it?

Yes, said the lady who was the city manager, it was a wonderful difficult time, I think, the best day of my life, I was in my room, sitting at the table and waiting, expecting an urgent visit at any moment, looking alternately at the clock and at the door that would open any minute now, but suddenly the tiled floor began to vibrate very gently in a spot near the table, naturally I thought that it might be a mild earthquake beginning slowly, but everything else remained still except for that one place on the floor, from which now a loose tile hopped, jumped up with a smacking sound and fell down again beside the hole thus created, and suddenly some furry, hairy thing pushed its way out of the hole thus created, so naturally I thought first of all that some strange animal might be surfacing in my room, but then quite unambiguously a head, an actual head . . .

You're quite right, City Manager, I heard Jagusch saying now, because of course, Madam, the water eventually began to rise up even farther, to a height of ten centimeters, and the stench, which was naturally also rising, then attained a height of two meters, as a result of which the people had to put on so-called stench masks, despite the heat, and the marketing and sales of those stench masks brought the rubber merchants in the city such a windfall that they're still living off it today, quite apart from the extra trade in the just-as-urgently-needed rubber boots people were buying because of the water that was climbing higher and higher, since then our rubber merchants have been the richest people in the city, with the most elegant villas at the edge of town, including this house with its garden, if I'm not mistaken; it belonged to a rubber merchant who then sold it to Mr. Diabelli.

It got colder and colder that summer, and one day it really did begin to snow, replied Jacksch, the district heating plants were naturally completely snowed in, even the entire north city was covered with ice, and all the factories had to shut down, it was a cold snap the likes of which we've never experienced even in the deepest winter, and against which we were all utterly helpless, and the worst thing was that we didn't have enough stoves, let alone enough firewood or other fuel, admittedly I was able to procure what was probably enough firewood for the members of my family, as you can imagine, but it proved impossible for me to find a proper stove anywhere, whereas some other people I know were able to get a stove, but it was impossible for them to find wood, coal, or other fuel for it anywhere, and so the entire city froze that summer, although many people had a stove or fuel at their disposal, almost no one had both a stove and fuel, whereas, Jacksch explained, if only those people who had fuel but no stove had gotten together with the people who had a stove but no fuel, then no one would have had to freeze, but all the people, said Jacksch, who was starting to sweat in the heat of the summer night from the effort that the verbal insertion of that past winter into the summer night was costing him, froze as never before in their lives, precisely because those people who had a stove but no fuel at their disposal were suddenly engaged in the bitterest of feuds with those people who had fuel but no stove, because every human being who had a stove but nothing to put in it to make heat hated every fellow human being who, to be sure, had fuel but no stove, hated him for not burning his fuel but just leaving it lying around and not wanting to hand it over even for a good price because he was still hoping to get a stove from somewhere, in vain, naturally, and every human being who had sufficient fuel but no stove in which to burn it hated every fellow human being who, to be sure, had a stove but no fuel to put in it, hated him for not using his stove but just leaving it standing around and not being willing to hand it over even for a good price because he was still hoping to get fuel from somewhere, in vain, naturally, so that, in a word, said Jacksch on that hot summer night, the people in the city in those days could have smeared both their stoves and their fuel in their hair, for all the good it would have done them, and nothing would have changed—that's how it was, City Manager, wasn't it?

Yes, I really hadn't expected that, I heard the city manager reply, all at once the hole in my floor contained the head of my urgently awaited visitor, whom I had previously been expecting to come through the door, just imagine!

Don't believe a word he says, I heard the building inspector say to the proctologist's wife, it was hot and humid, you'll remember, the water got higher and higher, and as you can imagine it was of course futile to pump away even a liter of water, because the same amount of water that was pumped away rose up again immediately from the ground. And all the water that actually should have run off down the naturally occurring slopes in our city didn't flow away of its own accord, that was the craziest thing I ever saw: *a large, downward sloping plane on which the water stood absolutely still, without running off*, just imagine that, young man, said the building inspector turning toward me.

And then what happened? I asked.

I don't know what you mean, said the building inspector, people just got used to it, eventually.

But it must have gone on somehow, and then it must have somehow come to an end, I said.

I told you, replied the editor, the referee, who was standing alone in the middle of the playing field, blew his whistle at first to get the game started again, but after he noticed that his whistling wasn't accomplishing anything, he called off the game prematurely and went into his room, at which point there was no holding back the spectators, they stormed the empty field.

No, I said, that's not what I meant, whereupon a man by the name of Zerbst, an Assistant Professor of Anthropology I happened to know superficially, who had been wanting to say something this entire time but had never gotten a chance, turned to me and said: I know what you're getting at, *because the dog had already been buried so much earlier, so to speak, the cause lay further back . . .*

You be quiet right now, the town planner interrupted him angrily, keep your mouth shut about a buried dog! We don't bury dogs here! What do dogs have to do with it?

A dog would really have been out of place back then, said the city manager, who had turned to me, because finally, after his head had broken through the floor, the rest of my visitor's body bored its way upward, shaking all over, that's what you meant, isn't it? and naturally more floor tiles had to go flying so my guest could finally push himself all the way up to where I was, whereupon the happy welcome proceeded, each of us beaming with joy, and everything else taking its natural course. But what do you think the first thing my visitor said to me was—just guess!

He said: I just found it too uncomfortable to climb up to you by way of the stairs, so I came directly through the floor!

Yes, the buffet, it must be emphasized, was really first class and substantial, but this should only be mentioned in passing:

That's fantastic, just look! What's that? Ox-throats, maybe?

So flaky and crunchy on the outside, but so light and fluffy, almost foamy on the inside.

I'd call it fleecy instead.

How do they do it, how can they make sure it always turns out that way?

That's easy, first of all you hang it up—by the hind legs, to be precise—until it's almost stopped wriggling, and then the head—as soon as it sticks its head out of the shell—you catch it quick as lightning in a noose, pull it out as far as possible and cut it off,

(she interrupted this graphic explanation very briefly to take a bite of carrot),

and then—and this is really the most important part—you have to let it hang for a few more days and, if possible, bleed out completely, otherwise it simply doesn't work!

Then you lay it on its back, added the hospital architect, who was standing nearby and was just in the process of taking apart one of the giant artichokes, and remove the lower shell with a long pointed knife—in fact, that's what you have to do before anything else!

No, no, replied Mrs. Jacksch, who was just then biting the head off a piece of asparagus that was almost three-quarters of a meter long, I do it completely differently, and much more expediently, actually, as follows: first you have to hold it so that it can't move anymore, look, like this (now she sucked dry several asparagus stalks),

because if you hang it up first, as you say, then it can still move, you see, but it shouldn't be able to move at all! Yes, and then you stab, added Assistant Professor Zerbst, who was peeling a pickle, then you stab down through the ribs with a long pointed knife, down, of course, not up, as you suggest, in any case right under the neck, and only then do you hang it up to drip dry, of course after you've pulled the knife out! Yes, you're really making a very big mistake by hanging it up right away, because then it's still moving too violently and causes all sorts of unnecessary difficulties!

But you're forgetting the most important thing, said Schwarz-kopf, who was pursuing a fully-grown porcini, stabbing at it with his fork, to finish the process you still have to hang it up, from the anus to the snout! If you don't do that, then I really see no hope for you!

The proctologist's wife proved to be well versed in dealing with difficult endive heads, you just take it by the wings with your left hand, she said, then you bend the neck back like this, without damaging the skin! (The large lettuce heart she had been eyeing half the evening now finally slipped into her oral cavity.)

And you, Johanna asked, lamenting my insistent silence during the dispute carried on by the public employees of our city, how were things with you during that wonderful difficult time?

Back then, on one of those days several years ago, I replied, I arrived here in this city on a very early morning train, and immediately afterwards got stuck here, haven't managed to get away again to this very day, although originally I'd intended to stay here for only a very short time. (I spoke of a time I had tried in vain to put behind me, a time when I, in my own assessment above all, had become a faltering and superfluous creature and had completely lost my self-esteem.)

What caused you to get stuck here? she asked.

I had arranged to meet my girlfriend in the city, I replied, but she wasn't here, she was nowhere to be found, I kept on looking for her, but she had disappeared without a trace, though I've always kept on looking, even up to a few minutes ago, and so I've been stuck here searching until today.

I don't think, Johanna said, that people disappear without a trace, maybe she just left you, and you're talking yourself into believing that she disappeared without a trace because you can't bear to think you were abandoned by her. Or maybe she disappeared without a trace because she thought her absence would be easier for you to bear if she disappeared without a trace instead of telling you to your face that she was leaving? How did you first notice that she'd disappeared? asked Johanna, and then asked me to tell her exactly.

We had only been separated for a short time, I replied, she'd come to this city in order to do some research for a study she was writing, while I had gone into retreat far away in order to finish composing some music. We agreed on a very definite day to meet again here in this city in order to go away together on a long trip we'd been planning for some time. Finally, then, the day had come, in the meantime it had started to snow. I arrived at seven o'clock in the morning after a long night on the train in a snowstorm, and it was still snowing heavily. Naturally, I went immediately to 68 Gustav Mahler Street, where she was living, and at last I was standing at the front door of the building and I rang the bell, but nothing happened. I kept on ringing, but there was no response. At last I heard slowly shuffling steps coming in the direction of the door from the inside stairwell, finally I thought, and shook off the summer snow. Then I heard a key turning in the front door lock and saw the heavy door open slowly with a squeaking sound, I raised my hands to take my girlfriend in my arms again at last, but then I stopped, startled, because what I saw was profoundly confusing to me.

What was it then? asked Johanna.

Standing in the open front door—you aren't going to believe this—was the Lord Mayor of the city, whose face I recognized from the newspapers.

What was he doing in that building at that time of day? asked Johanna.

I asked myself that too, I replied, maybe he still had a secret apartment there from the days before he was mayor, but that wasn't the problem—I was worried that I had mistakenly awakened him by ringing his doorbell and started to apologize for having done so. But he answered: you must be mistaken, because no one has rung my bell in a long time. Which button had I pressed? I showed him the button. Well of course that's not my button, he explained, and showed me his button. Did you press the right button? he asked then. Of course, I answered. Then be so good as to press that button again, if you're so certain, he ordered me, and so I pressed my button again. Press it harder, he said to me, press it harder. You always have to push it right in! I pressed as hard as I could, but there was no response. You probably think, he said then, that you just need to keep on pressing a button to make something happen? And if I thought that I had awakened or could awaken him of all people by ringing a bell, then I would have to get up earlier in the morning than he did, because he almost never slept—not that he couldn't sleep, but because he didn't want to. He called it an outrageous slander, accusing him of sleeping. You must have been dreaming, letting your imagination run away with you to think that I of all people was asleep—whereas you yourself have obviously slept through quite a few things in your day, he shouted. So please resume pressing now, yes, don't waste your time, press properly, always as hard as you can, and by the way you could have pressed my own button for hours, I disconnected the bell years ago, he said in parting, and then he disappeared into the drifting snow there in the center of the city. Naturally I kept on pressing, and naturally in vain, I stood in front of the locked entrance to the building pressing that button for hours, until I finally gave up. Two hours later I came back again to resume my efforts, but now the house wasn't there anymore, it was simply gone, vanished. Numbers 66 and 70 were still there, but number 68 was missing. Where is house number 68? I asked the inhabitants of Gustav Mahler Street. What? 68! No one knew anything about a 68—I had a terrible time explaining to the people what I meant. 68, they finally said, 68, oh yes, there hasn't been a house there for ages. But just two hours ago I myself was standing in front of it, I told them, referring to my encounter with the mayor. Torn down, they replied, it was only just torn down, and they showed me Caterpillar tracks not quite covered by the snow.

Don't you think you might have been at the wrong address? asked Johanna.

No, no, I replied, quite the opposite, because then of all times I was closer to her than I've ever been since.

You'll have to explain that to me in more detail, said Johanna.

So I turned around, I said, wanting to leave town again; but then I suddenly saw her walking on the other side of the street, turning down an avenue that ran through the fields of snow towards the train station, and having seen her, I stood motionless—though not without casting a happily hopeful glance at her gently swaying figure moving through the rows of trees—until I saw that she was all ready to leave on a trip, exactly as arranged, that she was having a hard time carrying two large suitcases, and so I thought, well, I guess we'll still be going away together today on that trip we've been planning for so long, and naturally I was already looking forward to using all the different means of public transportation at our disposal, and so I finally began to run after her, of course I wanted to cross over to her side of the street to help her carry her luggage, but I was prevented from doing so by the traffic that suddenly seemed very busy at that intersection. Unfortunately, she hadn't seen me, so she continued walking purposefully along the avenue, without turning around, and only then did I succeed in crossing the street and hurrying after her as quickly as I could, already out of breath, until in the middle of the road, I can't explain it, she had, there's no other way to put it, you know, because it was impossible that she could already have reached the station that was still miles ahead of us, *she had vanished into thin air, or become invisible,* you know, simply gone, yes, and even her footsteps in the freshly fallen snow on the sidewalk simply stopped where she had disappeared, didn't continue either doubled back or sideways, there were only two long wide fresh imprints from the suitcases she had put down, yes, at that point of her life everything about her that could have left any visible traces had come to an end. Of course I ran as quickly as I could to the train station, in case she had somehow managed to get there anyway, but there wasn't any sign of her, I asked conductors, linemen, signalmen, engineers, etc., but no one knew a thing.

And you never found her again? You've never seen her, met up with her, to this very day? asked Johanna.

No, I replied.

Well, you may not have *met* up with her, said Johanna, but I do think you *made* her up. Your girlfriend probably never existed—at least not in the way you wanted her to. And when you finally realized that she'd never been the way you always wanted, and because everything in your lives was quite different from the way you wanted to see it, you probably convinced yourself that she disappeared so that you could begin to look for her, and your search has not only become a habit, but also an excuse for a great deal of conscientious carelessness in your life. Since then, you've been searching for something that never existed and never will exist, and that's your excuse for why you've been stuck here in this city ever since.

But I really did experience everything exactly as I've told you, I replied.

Yes, I'll gladly believe you, said Johanna, because even reality is often a good invention.

We looked at each other for a long time, and I had a deeper and deeper desire to be close to Johanna, which closeness seemed so difficult for me to attain, I allowed my fingertips to glide lightly over her cheeks, very carefully, distanced thus by the width of our skin our eyes became better acquainted, all the knots between us were straightened out, and I found that her doubts about my own skeptical credulity inspired my confidence; I still wanted to say something, how lovely the quiet was, in this darkness punctuated by Chinese lanterns, or something like that (the mixture of dance music and guests' conversation became in my ears an irregularly beating hissing sound, like some Bacchanalian silent film about opera), but the sentences that I hadn't yet spoken were already being collected by her open lips brushing over my face;

then I felt like I was standing on the bank of a river, and all at once the rushing of the water had started to stutter!

There was great excitement now at the buffet:

Do pay attention now, quickly! I heard someone call.

What is it? people asked.

Don't you see there, the little truffle, look how it jumps!

Be so kind as to look more closely before making such confident assertions, will you? That's no truffle, it's a Brussel sprout!

Let's not quibble, can't you see it bounding away?

Yes, and now it's starting to flutter!

Yes, it's lifting off, with a hovering flight like a, like a death's-head moth!

Quickly! Faster, you can still catch it!

Oh! Too bad! Already gone. Too late.

Well well, it's always surprising how nimble something like that can be! Don't you think?

The painter Florian Waldstein was sitting the same way as before, leaning back comfortably in his wicker chair, he had just *shut his eyes*, this was known to be the position he took when he was longing to have a *conversation*. I went over to him, sat down in the wicker chair that was still free beside him, he noticed me without opening his eyes and recognized me immediately; closed eyes increase the capabilities of sensory perception considerably, he said.

I closed my eyes.

Behind the drawn curtain of my eyelids I saw and heard the party quite differently, at first much more powerfully, but then it suddenly became a sort of costume party, I couldn't recognize the guests in person, couldn't differentiate between them at all, because they all had the same frames fastened to their faces, and were wearing tall rubber boots that reached up high over their thighs, or else they had pulled darkly colorful and shining rubber skins over their entire bodies. Their movements were suited to their disguises: slippery, clumsy, stumbling and limping over the dance floors, swaying unevenly, hissing and hesitant, indeed, the people seemed to be connected by some sort of hooks that must have been attached invisibly to each of their costumes, they dragged each other along, pushed each other around stamping their feet, couldn't get free of each other, until finally they had gathered together into a great undulating heap of bodies suspended under the night sky, tethered ever more tightly to the dark blue horizon, which gradually rolled them up, squashing and crushing them in the process, and then rolled them out again, pumping the ball back up to its original size, and then inflating it further, almost to the bursting point.

Do you see all that too? I asked the painter, who, while fully confirming my observations, now drew my attention to a very particular spot in the farthest corner of the densely rustling garden.

Right at the back, he said, do you see, shimmering out between the waving bushes, creeping toward us? yes, I replied, and now also in the creaking underbrush, rustling, crackling, now crashing around, bursting forth, do you see those, what should I call them, horns, I think, or maybe they aren't horns?

Yes, they are horns, replied the painter, and now do you see also that huge head emerging between the cracking twigs and branches?

Yes, I replied, and now the entire front thorax or upper part of the body is pushing through as well, all white, sparkling at us white as snow!

Yes, white as snow, confirmed the painter, that much could have been foreseen, and now it's shining, its entire body nearly revealed, steaming and absolutely white! But that's, I said, what should I call it, maybe a bull, yes, a huge, snow-white bull! I now saw the mighty snow-white bull coming from the farthest undergrowth of the garden, approaching the pile of partiers, still knotted together, still connected, dancing around, and at first the bull was slowly bounding, then more and more it was leaping quickly toward them, but not one of the guests—who in the meantime had been able to disentangle themselves again—noticed it, though it had already lowered its widely spread horns into an attacking position.

What's this going to lead to? I asked the painter. Keep calm, he replied, what do you care? as the bull was galloping more and more furiously toward the partiers, who, although they should have long since recognized the imminent danger, were still swaying happily back and forth, the people glanced up indifferently at the threat rushing toward them, didn't move, didn't take the slightest notice of it, as though their eyes were tied up with blindfolds that were invisible to an observer, but that nevertheless deprived the person wearing them of sight. We absolutely have to warn them, I whispered to the painter. I don't see the slightest reason why, he replied, as the monster was already preparing to take the first dancers on its horns, if these people, said the painter, aren't even able to react on their own to inevitabilities of this nature, it's definitely not our responsibility to warn them.

Then I saw the bull suddenly stop, stand still, its horns lowered as before in the same dangerously threatening position, but no, it didn't stab at the dancers, that surprised me, it didn't gore anyone at all, but just held its head there very calmly with the polished points of its horns aimed directly into the midst of the partiers.

Why doesn't it attack? I asked the painter, first it comes galloping along showing every sign of intending to do so, as though it wanted to take the entire night together with this summer party onto its horns and send them both whirling into outer space, but now it's just standing there like a cow at a locked gate! Wait a minute, answered the painter, patience, just a little patience, you're about to witness a spectacle that's really unparalleled, right away!

And then I saw something squirting out of the tips of the bull's horns under incredible pressure, yes, there was actually a stream of water shooting out of each of its two horn tips, as though it was a zoological water cannon on four legs, the bull sprayed first of all into the midst of the milling party crowd, scattering them, and then sprayed sideways at the individual people who had been sprayed away from the crowd and even at the people trying to flee from the streams of water, so that nothing remained dry, soon everything had been knocked over, was tumbling, was swept away and inundated.

That's fantastic! I called to the painter.

Yes, I heard Waldstein reply, but I didn't really expect anything different; after all, it had to happen some day.

Of course the people screamed, and as soon as they'd half staggered to their feet, they were sprayed down again.

It's a pity, I said to the painter, really a pity that it only sprays water. Why not glue or soft soap?

It can do all that too, answered the painter, and when it really gets going, it pisses the whole world full of castor oil!

Only now did I see the carbuncle-like flashing in the animal's eyes, which were bulging from its skull, engorged. Until a sudden crash shook me in my seat.

The big buffet in the center of the party had fallen over, and the guilty person had already been found, it was Jacksch the city gardener, typically it was Jacksch, once again very typically Jacksch, people called.

It's a pity you opened your eyes again, said the painter, who had noticed this without having raised his eyelids, of course you're going to miss the best part now . . .

City Gardener Jacksch was scolded and then splashed from champagne bottles that people had shaken thoroughly before uncorking them in his direction, someone brought over the garden hose too and wanted to give the gardener a good soaking, but of course the gardener had far more experience with garden hoses and was able to dodge the spray in time, so that all the people standing around him had suddenly got their clothing drenched and only the gardener himself remained partially dry.

No, that's not possible, I heard Waldstein say, he was still sitting beside me—naturally with his eyes still closed.

Do tell, I begged him, what do you see, tell me!

It's getting better and better! said the painter.

So tell me, I begged Waldstein again.

No, he responded, I'm not telling you anything, I won't say a thing to you, you have only yourself to blame for having opened your eyes so early before the main event!

I shut my eyes again immediately and tried to see something more, keeping close watch behind my eyelids, but no matter how tightly I squeezed them shut, I couldn't find anything else, there was nothing to see, only the lights of the party exploding on my retina in complementary colors.

But there's nothing at all to see, I said to the painter, who didn't answer me. Tell me, I begged him for the last time, what's there now, I've closed my eyes and still can't see anything!

Too late, replied Waldstein, everything is over, it just ended.

He opened his eyes, not wanting to be spoken to anymore.

Do you see that, said Kalkbrenner, taking me aside, all those heads over there that hit the ground and then jump up again?

No, I explained to the poet, those are just the heads of the male and female dancers in the empty swimming pool, and what you're seeing are their bodies bouncing up and down, the jumps they perform during their dance causes their heads to appear very briefly over the edge of the swimming pool and then vanish again.

But Kalkbrenner wasn't prepared to change his mind: our

heads, he said, are independent of us, they are beings over which we have no influence, they jump around with us, leap around, as you can see very clearly over there, and the only thing they have in common with us is that the personalities in them, personalities that are completely foreign and unknown to us, talk *about* us (and unfortunately not *with* us) and tell the most impudent jokes at our expense, look, over there . . . !

The longer I listened to Kalkbrenner, the more clearly I saw the transparent figures he was talking about, throwing around the inflated heads of the party guests. The only thing that might succeed now and then, Kalkbrenner continued, would be to outwit one or even more of the personalities that occupy our heads, about whom we know nothing other than the fact that they ignore us, to trick them into finally meeting us . . .

Then I saw Anton Diabelli go up to his guests, gesturing that he had something important to say, asking for silence.

How happy he was that everyone had been enjoying themselves so far, he said, then he went on to say that the highpoint of the evening had not yet come, but that it would be happening very soon now, so he asked all the guests to gather in the salon in the house, adjoining the garden, where they would soon hear a concert that promised to be excellent.

Meanwhile, the salon had been turned into a proper little concert hall, a grand piano on the stage at the front, the usual seating as arranged for such an occasion at the back, the guests streamed into the house, took their seats, not without having fought for the ones they thought were best and now word slowly got out that Diabelli had succeeded in engaging the well-known pianist Schleifer, who would appear at any moment.

The music critic Pfeifer was also there among the guests, and a great number of music enthusiasts had gathered around him in order not to miss any of his knowledgeable explanations and opinion-forming commentaries: originally, I heard him explain to his attentive listeners that this piano concert was not meant to have been performed by Schleifer, but by Schläfer, but Schläfer had been unable to come for some reason and asked Schleifer to stand in for him because Schleifer always stands in when something goes wrong, I heard Pfeifer explain. Schleifer, by the way, was one of the few pianists who allowed themselves to play an evening concert without gloves, of course this was purely a matter of taste, but most other pianists naturally preferred to play *with* gloves, ranging from the most delicate kid gloves to thick rubber gloves to fur-covered winter mittens, said Pfeifer.

People sat quietly and expectantly in the salon, everyone was waiting eagerly for Schleifer, where is Schleifer? was heard asked many times, when will he finally come, it's already late and we want to get home again, and when the artist's door to the stage opened all of them probably thought at last, but it wasn't Schleifer who came out, a servant walked out to face the audience instead, naturally the disappointment was great, the crowd didn't hold back at all, grumbling loudly, the servant tried to explain to the audience that Schleifer had unfortunately forgotten his belt at home or some such thing, however he absolutely needed a belt to perform this piano concert and was asking if someone in the esteemed audience could help out by lending him a belt.

The people were, of course, astounded, quite rightly, and were whispering to one another that never before, according to Pfeifer's comments on this new precondition, had Schleifer needed a belt to perform one of his concerts, and yet now suddenly, gloves, yes, but not a belt, I heard people calling, and they let the servant disappear again without having achieved anything.

Finally Schleifer himself came out and was naturally greeted with thunderous applause and naturally he seated himself at the piano and was about to play, but the piano was still closed, Schleifer got up to open the grand piano properly, but it didn't work, not even the keyboard cover could be raised.

It's locked, I heard Schleifer call, the piano is still locked, he explained to the audience, and he couldn't possibly play on a locked piano, he needed the key. Hello, I heard Schleifer call, the key, where is the key? Then the servant came running, but he didn't understand, key, people called to him from the audience, the key!

What kind of key? asked the servant shaking his head, he didn't have any key, he tried to explain, well, yes, he had the key to the salon, but why would anyone suddenly want the salon key again now? the salon was open, wasn't it? or was he supposed to lock the salon up again?

No, they didn't want the salon key, I heard Schleifer explain to the servant, they wanted the piano key.

What? asked the servant, the piano key? no, of course he didn't have that, as far as he knew there was no piano key, this was the first he'd heard of it. What should we do? I heard Schleifer ask, he turned to the audience again, does any one of you perhaps have the piano key? he asked.

The members of the audience searched through their pockets, pulled out their key rings, soon all you could hear was the manifold jingling of key rings, people tried a few keys on the piano, but none of them fit, and soon they gave that up too.

Fortunately one of the guests stood up, he happened to be a locksmith, as he informed Schleifer, and if he, Schleifer, absolutely wanted him to, he would be able to open the piano for him, he had a skeleton key with him.

I saw Schleifer sigh with relief, he reached into one of his pants pockets, presumably to take out a handkerchief to wipe the sweat from his brow, but it wasn't a handkerchief that came out, it was a key, here, the key, called Schleifer, here is the right key at last, beaming with pleasure he held up the piano key so that we all could see it, found at last, but the locksmith had already broken open the piano, Schleifer didn't need a key anymore, he sat down at the piano and began to play, even the unpleasant belt problem from before had long since been forgotten, but then Schleifer suddenly interrupted his playing.

He'd thought he would be able to do it without a belt, but as it turned out it just wasn't possible, as he now noticed, especially for coping with this and that coming passage he absolutely needed a belt, and wouldn't someone from the audience be so kind as to help him out?

But no one in the audience seemed to be wearing a belt, suspenders, they called up to Schleifer, suspenders, yes, won't suspenders do the job? but Schleifer wanted nothing to do with suspenders, then finally in the back row the fat city gardener Jacksch made it known that he was wearing a belt, undid his belt, and let it be passed up to the front. But make sure to give me back my belt after the concert, I heard City Gardener Jacksch call up to Schleifer, otherwise his pants would fall down, and he didn't know how he would get home after the party without losing his pants, he couldn't possibly hold up his pants with his hands the whole way because he had to carry two heavy bags with important documents in them that were indispensable for covering up the building scandal regarding the large greenhouse he worked at every day, and it wasn't really possible to hold up his pants and to carry the bags at the same time.

The fat city gardener's belt was, as you can imagine, too wide for

Schleifer, wide, much too wide, I heard Schleifer say, an extra hole will have to be bored through here, now they would need a sharp object, if possible a drill.

But where would they find a drill all of a sudden, one lady did have her knitting with her, she had wanted to finish knitting something during the party in order to make good use of her time, and observing that you have to start thinking of the winter during the summer, I saw her hand the pianist a knitting needle, which of course proved to be much too blunt, with such a blunt knitting needle they would never have been able to bore through the hard leather of the belt.

As it turned out, the fat Kalkbrenner was also a belt-wearer and wanted to place his at their disposal.

Oh be quiet, they hissed back at him, don't you see that you're also much too fat to be able to have a belt that would fit the pianist.

What? I heard Kalkbrenner reply to that, so he was fat, that was news to him, he was hearing people slander him in that fashion for the first time, because really he was very slim, yes sir! extremely slim, it's just that all his pants were much too wide, so that he was forced to assume his apparent girth, unfortunately, in order to fill out these much-too-wide pants.

Then I saw Pfeifer fiddling around with his waistband, yes, he too was wearing a belt, as it turned out, which he undid, if hesitantly and with a hint of resentment, and handed it to the pianist on the podium, who immediately tried it on, yes, it fit, Schleifer looked quite respectable in it, spoke of it as the only correct solution and resumed playing the piano at last.

The page turner was sitting motionless to Schleifer's left, leaning back comfortably with his legs stretched out, I heard Pfeifer explaining the page turners' dilemmas to the music enthusiasts sitting around him, on whose faces was written a deep need to have their horizons broadened: Musicians often play such fast pieces that their page turners aren't able to follow the music. The musicians should be so kind as to play slower pieces or to play these very fast pieces more slowly, the page turners have repeatedly requested, so that they, the page turners, can follow along, but of course the musicians wouldn't agree to that, so they came to the following interim solution, Pfeifer explained: when the pianist nods, with his head of course, then the page turner is supposed to turn the page, not before, and also not too long after.

Now Schleifer was quite plainly nodding as he played, bobbing his head up and down, it seemed to be the signal, but the page turner remained motionless, as before. Turn! I heard Schleifer scream at the page turner, will you please turn the page! He went on playing anyway, stamping his feet, whereupon the page turner finally—naturally much too late—rose from his comfortable position on the chair, bending his body over the keyboard toward the open book of music and starting to reach his outstretched hand toward the page that was to be turned, but Schleifer had beaten him to it, he had already turned the page himself when one of his hands was free for a fraction of a second. Did you see that now? I heard Pfeifer ask the people sitting around him rhetorically, and of course you have to put yourself in the position of the page turner. Schleifer, that is, Pfeifer explained, as you can see for yourself, is one of those pianists who knows how to lend gestural emphasis to the musical expression of the piece he's playing through a whole variety of bodily movements, and so the page turner presumably misunderstood Schleifer's nodding as belonging to those expressive movements that accompany the flow of his music choreographically.

I saw the page turner still standing bent over beside the playing pianist, and with the hand he had previously stretched out in vain, and which had remained in that position, he reached for the page that Schleifer was now playing and turned it, even though it wasn't time for that yet.

Don't turn! I heard Schleifer roar at his page turner, stamping on the floor, without interrupting his piano playing in the least, don't turn, turn it back right now! But the page turner, who needed about ten times as long to get up from his chair as he needed to sit down and lean back again, was now busy stretching out his legs, and Schleifer had a hard time turning back the page himself without interrupting his playing.

Now, did you see that? I heard Pfeifer offering his expert interpretation of this occurrence to his followers as well, that was bad of course, but even in this instance one has to try to understand the page turner's mistake from his perspective. To wit, Schleifer has, and I saw it myself, said Pfeifer, in the course of the body movements that accompany his piano playing, carried out a new movement that was confusingly similar to a head-nod, which was then interpreted by the page turner as a head-nod on Schleifer's part, and so of course he turned the page right away, you see. But at any rate, it's progress for the page turner to have turned a page at all, I've seen page turners, Pfeifer went on talking shop, who haven't turned anything at all, nothing, never anything at all, but who always just sit there quietly. And many page turners, Pfeifer explained to his followers in a heated tone, approaching passion, are of the opinion—which in my view is not at all mistaken—that the musician should follow the page turner rather than vice versa, whether the page turner is a man or a woman, each page that the page turner opens should be kindly played by the musician, for why else should the page turner turn pages if the turned page isn't going to be played there and then, yes, the page turners have had enough of the oppression of musicians once and for all, you see, and so when the page turner nods, the pianist should turn the page, absolutely!

Mr. Pfeifer, I said to the critic then, listen, what will you do if some day the musicians strike against the page turners? Just imagine, you're sitting at a concert, waiting eagerly for the musicians to appear, the artist's door to the podium opens, but instead of the musicians coming out, it's the page turners, which would be quite a surprise. How fortunate, Pfeifer replied, that you're not the only composer we have, since, especially in such an unlikely case, we would certainly have to rely on those far more competent composers, who—probably in great contrast to you—would be quite capable of writing real and usable music for page turners.

Schleifer's concert piece had gradually come to an end, the pianist bowed, and naturally received friendly applause, but above all, people were now effusively congratulating Pfeifer for having kindly offered the service of his excellent belt, with the help of which everything had become possible, people said how moving the music had been, thanks, that is, to Pfeifer's intervention; many expressed the view that the more tightly Schleifer had buckled Pfeifer's belt, the more convincing his piano playing became, and that the pianist should have played not just the second, but also the first part, that is, the entire concert, wearing the reviewer's belt. You were absolutely outstanding once again, the people called out to Pfeifer, who attempted, making a show of great humility, to pass on to Schleifer, as his due, at least the lesser part of the tributes offered him: he spoke of Schleifer's partially masterful piano playing, of his laudably elegant restraint in the placement of certain particular accents, yes, that was art, through which a human being is changed, said the art critic, you could actually see the people changing, some rose above themselves, getting taller and taller, so that the salon ceiling at times seemed much too low, except that in the next moment people become very short, so that they all but disappeared, only then to suddenly get very fat, an enormous expansion of their girths, so that the salon suddenly seemed much too narrow, because the listeners were all pushing one another away to get more room for themselves, and finally, toward the end of the concert, the audience had all gotten very thin, become barely recognizable gossamer-thin lines crossing out the concert as soon as the last note had died away, and there wasn't a listener here who hadn't been deeply moved by the piece in one way or another. Going on to talk about Schleifer's lack of experience with certain articles of clothing, Pfeifer could be heard to conclude that the artist had unfortunately experienced some difficulties in the first part of the concert, which, however, had sorted themselves out in the second part of the concert, namely when the pianist had suddenly stopped playing.

Again I saw Anton Diabelli stand up in front of his guests, indicating with gestures that he had something important to say, getting their attention, he had just succeeded, he said, in convincing Schleifer to play something else, and as you perhaps knew, Schleifer was not only an outstanding pianist, he could also play a considerable number of other instruments as well, mainly winds, and, he thought, the viola as well, and so he would now play, he thought, a little brass-band music. While the guests took their seats again, Schleifer reappeared and announced his encore to the crowd, which was now quieting down relatively quickly—they didn't want

Schleifer anymore, many of them said, they wanted Pfeifer—he would, he said, play an excerpt from a sonata that could be played either on the clarinet or the viola, accompanied by the piano, and accompanying himself on the piano, he would perform those sections on the clarinet that he felt seemed more suitable to the work performed on the clarinet than on the viola, but those sections that he felt were more suitable for the viola than the clarinet he would naturally perform on the viola; those sections, however, where he could not decide in favor of either of these two instruments, he would perform on both instruments simultaneously *unisono* or would dispense with them altogether. He sat down at the piano to begin right away, to get the introductory measures of the piano accompaniment behind him, and I no longer know if it was Brahms's Sonata for Clarinet or Viola in F Minor, opus 120/1 or the one for Viola or Clarinet, opus 120/2 in E flat major, in any case everyone was eagerly awaiting the entry of either the clarinet or the viola when suddenly the listeners got restless, where's his clarinet? the people asked each other, there wasn't the slightest trace of a viola either, in fact, Schleifer didn't have either of the two instruments anywhere visibly within reach, probably forgot them at home too, some of the listeners feared, and then he'll want to borrow both from Pfeifer.

Quiet, hissed those who were of a different opinion, he probably has both hidden away somewhere close to him and will get them out in due course as required.

Then we could clearly hear Schleifer's clarinet entering, even though he didn't have a clarinet with him—with exemplary embouchure on the mouthpiece, sounding forth from his head, ringing forth, the calm and elegant movement of the extended, wide-ranging melody, he seemed to produce a clarinet tone that testified to an excellent breathing technique, somewhere in the region of his mouth or throat, in any case blowing it out of his thorax, and the sound that he produced had a tonal quality easily as rich as that produced on a traditional clarinet, and I think the clarinetless Schleifer outdid every other clarinetist who blew on a traditional clarinet, particularly with his polished, balanced tone. Of course the audience couldn't grasp that, no, it wasn't right at all, stop, they called, they felt deceived, this charade had to stop right away, where was his clarinet, the people called out, he's got one hidden somewhere, we won't stand for that! When the unrest wouldn't let up, Schleifer interrupted his playing and turned to the doubting listeners. Do you always have to know that an instrument or some other auxiliary device is being used or is at least in the vicinity before you're prepared to admit something? he asked the audience, gradually getting them calmed down, it's well known, he said, that human beings, before they understand something, grope around it so long, squeezing it until they crush it, that in the end there's nothing left to be understood.

You're just trying to divert our attention from the fact that you, in actual fact, can't really play the clarinet, the audience called out to him. They handed Schleifer a clarinet from the dance band with the request that he be so good as to demonstrate his skill. Feeling snubbed, the musician refused the instrument that was offered to him, you mean you still don't understand? he said, I can do a clarinet without needing a clarinet—if a clarinet isn't necessary for me, what can I possibly do with one?

The fact that he could produce the clarinet tones within himself and bring them out without having to use the auxiliary device of an actual clarinet obviously wasn't acceptable to them, the listeners, as he could see, explained Schleifer, but even you will slowly have to get accustomed to the idea that with the passage of time, the use of musical instruments will become less and less common, more and more frequently musicians will refrain from the use of musical instruments, since they will have finally recognized that they are unnecessarily hampered by having to operate these devices, upon which they grow increasingly dependent, and as you can see, even listeners become unpleasantly distracted from the actual content of music by these dubious contraptions. He asked the guests to keep listening, to surrender themselves to the music, he spoke of ridiculous formalities bordering on the superficial, to which no importance should be attached in art and especially not in music, and he continued to play, working through a section on the piano alone for a long time.

He has begun, I heard Pfeifer explaining Schleifer's methods with an unmistakably ironic undertone, winking at his followers, to set up an entire symphony orchestra in which the use of musical instruments is strictly forbidden.

Finally, Schleifer let his invisible viola enter, a long, curved melody, lightly ornamented, arching continuously from one wall of the salon to another, that began to wrap itself ingratiatingly around the seated guests, and the violaless violist knew with utter conviction how to produce a more than perfect viola tone, surpassing every traditional viola, this time even Pfeifer was impressed by the performance, this man can do the violin although he has no violin, I heard him calling approvingly to his followers, and he found that to be worthy of imitation. Nevertheless, a majority of the guests were unprepared to understand even that, stop! they called, it's the same charade all over again, this time with the fiddle, we simply won't stand for any more, and they handed him a fiddle and bow from the dance band, here, a fiddle, now be so good as to play it.

Of course you hadn't noticed, said Schleifer, refusing the fiddle, that I wasn't playing the fiddle, but rather the viola, nothing can be accomplished with a fiddle in this piece, and if they wanted to force him to fiddle around with an instrument, they should be so good as to get him a viola. Of course they wanted to help him get a viola right away, but couldn't find one anywhere. See, said Schleifer after that, you don't have a viola that you could give me, but fortunately we can all dispense with that, because I can do the viola without a viola, and now you can finally see how good it is that I can do the viola without being dependent on an actual viola, because if we had to rely on the possibility of a viola being present, the sonata couldn't go on. Schleifer wanted to continue making music, but the people wouldn't let him, they were muttering about it all being rigged and said they suspected some kind of malicious sabotage; finally Pfeifer, taking Schleifer's side with complete conviction, leapt up and said to the guests, this man is entirely right, because he, Pfeifer, had been preaching the same thing over and again in vain for the past twenty years: A musical instrument has always been first and foremost an unwieldy, unpractical appendage, and above all because of its mechanical limitations has always been a transitional, provisional device restricting the artistic will of the musician, not only completely inadequate for performing music in earnest, but also basically useless. We must, Pfeifer went on to explain, reach the point where we can finally produce the sounds of all musical instruments within ourselves, so that the last remnants of these tonally entirely unsuitable devices for producing musical sounds, whose appearance alone must instill horror in each and every honest musician, can be locked away in the museums. I declare, said Pfeifer, all musical instruments from this day forth to be abolished once and for all, and to anyone crossing my path who still wants to play something on an instrument for me, I can only say with a pitying smile, go home, throw your trumpet in the river, all I can tell you is to fire up your furnace and burn your mandolin without delay!

Wanting to acknowledge his good intentions, I heard Schleifer reply then to Pfeifer, but the ideas just expressed by the critic seemed to Schleifer completely inadequate, to put it mildly—narrow-minded and without an eye to the big picture. Because not only are musical instruments bothersome crutches that have to be thrown away, but audible notes and tones also do nothing but interfere with the pure experience of music, distorting it beyond recognition! Listen, said Schleifer to Pfeifer, hammering out a few loud chords on the keyboard, these unnecessarily jarring noises, these sounds, these so-called notes and melodies that we hear while listening to music, these don't have anything to do with the actual intent of music, and it's wrong to assume that the note, that notes themselves make up music—rather, these sounds that become audible when music is played are only an offensive acoustic excretory product that results from the performance of the content of music and in the process falsifies and destroys it! In future, Schleifer explained, all that matters will be that music can be experienced without the disruptive additional noise of these so-called notes and tones.

I remember how very quiet it got in the salon as Schleifer finished playing the sonata he had begun, demonstrating his concept of ideal music, no one had ever heard anything like it before, I saw the guests swaying calmly and silently to and fro on their seats, abandoning themselves to the silence of the sonata that was now completely enveloping them, listening to it with studious concentration, and although Schleifer was banging away at the keyboard up on the podium, not a sound could be heard. Listen—I heard Schleifer interpreting the piece of music on the side, to his listeners, as he performed it—this is how this sonata is supposed to sound, and not otherwise, and Pfeifer commented in agreement to his followers, only when we hear nothing, nothing at all, will we comprehend and understand music, listen!

I went out into the dark, abandoned garden for a while to clear my head.

Johanna was standing outside, deep in conversation with Florian Waldstein, who, when he saw me coming, retreated immediately to his wicker chair and began an intense observation of the night.

I think if you would only come closer and closer to me, I said to Johanna, I would be able to breathe properly again.

I worry, she responded, that you want to repeat your relationship from years ago, your relationship with your missing girlfriend, without whom you think you've been unable to find your way until now, with me. You surely know that this isn't possible. I don't want to become a product of your inventive imagination. Anyway, you can't just set up a comfortable little apartment for yourself in my heart, someplace you can retreat to whenever you don't happen to be enjoying your own company . . .

I wanted to go back into the salon, and saw through the glass door that Schleifer was just finishing the last bars of the silent sonata, eliciting the most spectacular, virtuosic silence from his instrument that I'd ever experienced, he was playing away *furioso* and had really worked up a sweat,

when the night air suddenly, oscillating gently around me, began to sound, a lightly vibrating hum had penetrated through to me from all around, or was it a singing of notes descending toward me from a height I would hardly have thought possible, and being scattered by the light wind that had just sprung up. I had the sensation of overlapping wandering clouds of notes and gather-

ing mists of tones that shifted into one another, surging forward and back, a very quiet, barely audible, devastatingly beautiful music, such as I had never experienced before, very high, but at the same time very low, agreeably subdued, slightly blurry gossamer-thin aerial chordal expanses, pieced together from the notes that had risen up from the landscape, from all the imaginable notes sounding in the region, I felt myself entirely enveloped in pulsating, flowing, continually regenerating sounds whose highest and lowest tonal levels were bent so far apart that they touched each other at the outer edges of tonality, or audibly crossed, only to bend apart again, oscillating into each other to form a different mass of sound. So the night then had become a spacious resonant balloon, to which the plain below was firmly lashed, it was pumped full of wind arpeggios ranging in sound from dark to sparkling, and then emptied again, a gradual hovering upwards that was accompanied by a continual slight dropping. After the chordal fog had been dismantled by the fluttering aerial trills sounding through the night, it fell over the park like a light breath from all directions, and at a very particular point, as I heard, swaying to and fro, collecting its individually shimmering tonal splashes, it then arranged itself into yet another never previously audible collection of sounds, which dispersed again soon afterwards in a singing with a very gentle tremolo. I felt the individual notes gliding tenderly over my skin through my head brushing against my entire body, flowing through it, a musical wind flooding through me that released unknown sensations and feelings in me that I thought for a moment might overwhelm me and that I couldn't name, it was a kind of endlessly expanding long and wide pulling or being pulled, I was being seized by a sort of dreamily happy sadness, I moved, no, I was being moved, I felt light, as though I was floating away, and then I was taken by an unspeakably sad joy.

I looked for the place from which this continually oscillating aerial song was originating, spreading itself out, hovering in all directions, getting a little louder and a little quieter, and to where it was then lightly blown back from everywhere it reached, so I went deeper and deeper into the farthest part of the garden at the back, where I soon reached the desired place. I was standing *on the shore of the small pond overgrown with reeds, and the sounds were rising up, funnel-shaped, from the water—or else they were spun by the wind into its wavering surface. I couldn't distinguish whether the music that was so penetrating me disappeared into me or rather I into it, whether I was being devoured by those sounds for which I would gladly have given up all the music and musicology that I had studied. And everything else too.*

So I was standing at the edge of this slightly stagnant-smelling pond full of fresh algae, abandoning myself to the beautiful music that made everything around it seem devastatingly ludicrous, anyone who could hear such music would have to stop doing anything else, the sounds were stronger than every imaginable argument to the contrary, and if those chords had had it in them to destroy me, or bring me to the point where I was no longer able to exist, I would have been the first to give myself up to this destruction, and with the most fervent devotion.

I wasn't alone for long, however, because the other guests too had heard and felt and had been captivated by this succession of notes hovering in the air, they approached slowly and carefully, taking cautious steps, as if they feared that any hasty movements or careless, disruptive noises might frighten away those edifices of sound in the landscape that until then had scarcely been imaginable, let alone audible, and by which even the coarsest people in the crowd were inexplicably moved. Then they all, we all, stood around that pathetic puddle of water in a peculiar unity, staring spellbound into the liquid, and in our paralysis were swiftly slowly captivated by an immeasurably clear intoxication of sound, an incalculably violent kind of tenderness that consigned us and all our failures and mutual hatreds to oblivion. Slowly the music got quieter and quieter, disappearing, sinking deeper and deeper into the water, from whose surface the last notes now hastily blew away, and soon all that could be perceived was a barely audible, not even humming, but a sort of long drawn-out murmuring, and finally complete quiet, and only in the mind did a melancholy echo persist, bent with the painful longing that had got stuck in the calm of that summer night.

The people detached themselves from the side of the pond, lifting their faces up again from the surface of the water as though they were rising up again from a collective descent, from a collective dream that had now just lifted off and sailed away.

I saw the people wandering helplessly through the park as before with slow careful cautious movements, seating themselves in expectant postures on the garden furniture in the vain hope that the phenomenon would return.

Johanna had been in a deep embrace with Florian Waldstein during the night music; so you did come back to me, I heard the happy painter say. But Johanna freed herself from him and said: No, because you've always treated me like a natural wonder which you happen to find moving, and nothing will ever change between us in the future. It frightens me to represent an irreplaceable work of art that you take for your own. You still just want to repeat our relationship of many years ago, without which you think you can't find your way, but you know that isn't possible.

Because the memory of you can never stop, I heard Waldstein say, and my thoughts of you can never again be taken from me, a life without you would cause me to gradually disappear into myself, until nothing is left.

You have so often, I heard Johanna reply, seen only a reflection of yourself when you've looked at me, so you never noticed that I've often looked back at you out of myself through the mirror image that you impose on me, without your ever meeting my gaze.

I will always hope that you'll come back to me some day, I heard Waldstein say.

My life when I was around you, I heard Johanna reply, was only a thin protective skin you wore to keep out an environment you considered unbearable. You took advantage of my existence in order to experience your happiness through me, a happiness that I was afraid to shatter because you spread yourself out wider and wider inside me, where there was nothing else but you.

No, I heard Waldstein say, trying to move Johanna's metaphor onto more sympathetic territory, I had already lost myself in you, so completely fallen in love with you, that soon you will no longer be able to find anything more of me in you, nor anywhere else.

Kalkbrenner, the poet, had taken out his pencil and notepad and had obviously begun to write a story, and I was attempting on a piece of notepaper to jot down from memory at least a few sequences of notes in their systematic succession and pitch from the phenomenon, its tone color was hopelessly indefinable anyway, since it was music performed on unknown, unmanufacturable instruments, a music that had to be thought. But not a single one of the notes or chords wanted to let itself be graphically arranged on the paper, and not because my memory was too weak, on the contrary, it's retained to this day a perpetual longing to hear that music again as soon as possible, and then if possible to hear it continually, but because the tones simply could not be put down on a surface like a piece of notepaper in the traditionally used two-dimensional system of representation, the notes and tones in my memory could only conceivably have been represented at different elevations in the space above and below the piece of notepaper and also around it in an endlessly extended three-dimensional spatial system of coordinates for musical notation and never on the piece of notepaper itself, which makes sense insofar as a music that moves in a dimension different from our traditional one, in the next highest or an even more distant dimension, would necessarily require at least the next highest dimension from our conventional flat writing surfaces for its notational representation. Presumably I was tempted to write a few such notes with my pencil in the air over my piece of notepaper, which may have caught the attention of the passing proctologist, the hospital architect, and Pfeifer the music critic; shaking their heads, they posed the question of the deeper meaning of my activity.

I'm trying, I replied, to note down the sounds by which I've been completely captivated and towards which I am capable of nothing but devotion, whereupon the proctologist, shaking his head in concern, began to speak of the typical symptoms of chronic addiction, and the hospital architect offered me a free stay in one of those institutions of his, which he described as works of art.

What do you have to say about it? I asked Pfeifer.

What?

What do you have to say about it?

About what?

Well, about that music we were all so moved by, I'm interested in your professional opinion as a music critic.

Which music do you mean, I don't hear any music? said Pfeifer.

No, I replied, not now, but a short while ago.

You mean Schleifer's performance, said Pfeifer, I've already adequately expressed myself about that, I've always been of the same opinion as him.

No, I don't mean Schleifer, but afterwards, you know, that very bright darkened trembling in the air just a few minutes ago!

A few minutes ago? asked Pfeifer, I really don't know what you mean, you must be mistaken, the dance band is long since gone, and there's not the slightest trace of Schleifer anywhere at all now . . .

The music that could suddenly be heard everywhere after the

piano concert, I explained to Pfeifer, that, what can I call it, that natural music, that indescribable stream, that flow, like a, like a . . .

Like a Kneipp cure, a hydropathic treatment combined with diet and rest, is that what you mean?

You know exactly what I mean, I said to Pfeifer, you just don't want to admit that language has failed you too. Excuse me, said Pfeifer, but now I really don't know what you're talking about, do you know what he means? he asked one of the people standing around him.

No, he didn't know either.

After Schleifer, I said once again, that oscillation in the air . . .

After Schleifer, you say, said Pfeifer, more music after Schleifer, after the great Schleifer, who has already jumped miles ahead of everything, you claim to have found other music worth mentioning? Did you hear anything else after the piano concert? Pfeifer asked one of the people standing around him.

No.

Or you?

No.

Or you? Hey! You there! No, not you, but you, yes you! What's your name again? What? Jacksch! Mrs. Jacksch, did you hear anything? No? You didn't either?

See, said Pfeifer then, Mrs. Jacksch didn't hear anything either.

Or you there, Pfeifer now called out to the town planner, you there, what did you hear? What did you say? What? Please repeat that! You aren't saying anything else, you say? You've already said everything, you say? I, however, heard nothing, listen to me, I heard nothing! Did you hear anything? What? You don't want to hear anything else now, you say? No, I'm not asking whether you want to hear something, no one wants to hear anything now, but

I'm asking you if you heard anything, that's what I want to know. No? Well, see now! Pfeifer said to me then, no one heard anything, no one knows what you're going on about!

Kalkbrenner had ended his story, he put his pencil back in his pocket and came over to me with the writing in his notepad, wanting to lend support to my musical opinion, actually no one else seems able to remember it, he said, and found that quite regrettable, so for that reason he found it advantageous to read aloud right then the story he had just finished writing, which dealt in detail with everything that the other guests now claimed to know nothing about.

No, they replied, and what he, Kalkbrenner, thought, they would probably rather think over some other time, now was not the time to consider it, reading a story was absolutely not called for now, and the guests started getting unruly, a reading would have to be stopped, oh please no story now, they called, but Kalkbrenner had already begun to read his story aloud, and it went something like this:

THE SINGING LAKES

One day, in the middle of the country, a little pond began to sing. All the people in the surrounding area were attracted by its pleasant sounds, sounds that enveloped and immobilized everything, they gathered around it and stared down into the singing water, captivated by the notes that rose up from the pond. The wind carried the music of the pond to the larger lakes in the country, whereupon there too all the people gathered on the shores of their lakes, staring down into the liquid music that rose from the many surfaces of the many bodies of water.

The chords could also be heard on the banks of the rivers, people had happily set up colorful tents on the islands in the rivers so that they could henceforth devote themselves exclusively to this music, and devote themselves to their devotion to it, because everything that had seemed most desirable in their lives was suddenly quite unimportant and had even become ridiculous in comparison with their devotion to the music, the music that would soon conquer and subjugate everything.

Via the rivers, the singing reached the oceans.

Now all people everywhere have settled on the shores of all their local stretches of water, in colorful tonal intoxication parties!

In time, the people want to penetrate ever deeper into the music of the waters, to go farther out into the musical water in their boats, just to be more completely absorbed into the sounds, to fathom the final secrets of the notes even as they themselves dissolve:

one after another they all plunge into the lakes, rivers, and oceans, are swept away, drown in the water, in the music.

And only a few remain alive:

The deaf, living in deserts, on the steppes and savannahs.

And then the story really got going, going into an extensive, detailed, and masterful description of the deserts, steppes, and savannahs and all their inhabitants, it was quite obvious that he was describing our own surrounding circumstances, and that was naturally too much, to be literally described by Kalkbrenner, stop, cried the people, we already know all that, plagiarism, screamed the proctologist, every word copied, cut this nonsense short immediately, but Kalkbrenner didn't stop, so the people tore his notebook away from him and ripped it up, and the gray early morning wind blew the scraps of his story through the park, but Kalkbrenner knew the story by heart and so kept on reading.

Now everything started to happen very quickly, moving to its confusing end, the memory of it in my head is only fleeting and hazy, as though my stacks of orderly thoughts were somehow scattered violently, thrown up in the air, I was carried away, I don't remember exactly how, but in any case, someone had brought a rope from somewhere, thrown it over the nearest good-sized bough on the biggest tree in the center of the garden, it looked like they were preparing for an execution, in any case I saw Jacksch coming out of one of the tool sheds behind the house carrying an axe, no, this axe is far too blunt for what we have in mind, I heard him say, they urgently needed tools that had been kept in good condition, he spoke of *otherwise possible, inevitably occurring*, strangely unlikely professional errors, you know, he said, some time ago, I think at least ten years ago, I was faced with the choice of either splitting this block of wood that was particularly difficult to split, or not splitting it, and naturally even then there was no question, as you can imagine, but to undertake a splitting, in fact a drastic splitting.

You're quite right, Jagusch called out to Jacksch, do go on!

Yes, go on, called the reporter, not so slowly, a little more fluently, if I might make that request!

Kalkbrenner, whose stomach was fastened to the rope hanging from the tree, didn't let that stop him from continuing his description of the desert-dwellers. Don't you see that you're interrupting Jacksch's story? said the reporter to the poet, give him a chance to say something too!

Go on, will you, Jagusch called out to Jacksch. So I was standing in front of the chopping block, said Jacksch, who with his free hand, while the pickaxe dangled from the other, indicated to the interested guests that they were to imagine a chopping block in front of him, the block of wood to be split was on the chopping block of course, here, you see, but as I said back then again and again, of course in vain, the circumstances weren't ideal, but in any case I knocked a wedge provisionally into the surface of the block of wood, so that the wedge, which was so bitterly necessary for all of us back then, stood upright on its own and didn't keep falling over, thus I had attained the most favorable starting position imaginable for driving the wedge through the block of wood with a single well-aimed blow with the broad side of the axe, bringing it down vertically on the head of the wedge, the most favorable starting position imaginable for finally being able to split the piece of wood, said Jacksch, who, swinging his axe through the air in front of him, tried to demonstrate the movement to the guests, who were straining to follow along, chopping apart the first light of morning, in which Kalkbrenner's body was caught like a big insect, he had been tied up and suspended in the hope that he would finally stop telling his story, won't you be quiet and let Jacksch continue? Jagusch screamed to the poet swinging around in the air, you could learn a lot from him.

The break of day, sticking to the night sky like a thick, furry coat of mildew, now called for my complete attention—first there were black cracks, and then these multiplied, getting lighter and lighter and spreading out at an astounding speed, and they now stood out silvery white, forming an ever more closely-woven net that was stretched through the night air all around and above us.

Soon the night will have crumbled completely and will form into early morning mist down here, I said to the reporter: when the first rays of sun creep through the holes in the sky net, you'll see, the last night lichen will fall from the clouds and flutter down and sink into the forests, which soon will be the only places left in this landscape where there's still any darkness, look, the last remaining streaks of night are already flying through the air in the form of swallows, you absolutely must report on all this in your newspaper!

Why don't you look over there instead, the reporter replied, drawing my attention back to Jacksch, don't look in the air, look at Jacksch, there's a lot more going on with Jacksch than meets the eye, I think the man is more than capable when left to his own devices, you know, I think everyone could learn a thing or two from him.

So do it, the people called out to Jacksch, get on with it!

Dull, much too dull, Jacksch called back, where can we find a grindstone, a whetstone right away, so that we can at least sharpen the axe a little . . . Stop talking about a whetstone, this isn't the time for sharpening, you'll be able to do it even without a whetstone, they replied, pointing at Kalkbrenner who was still wriggling in the air, still persisting in telling his desert story; just go and do it, they called to Jacksch, you don't have to take that nonsense from him, if I were you I wouldn't put up with it for long, Jagusch called, so go on and do it!

But Jacksch didn't do it, he just tested the sharpness of the axe again instead.

Now the air high up formed into little ponds that expanded into lakes and these soon flowed into each other, and the thick clouds were run through by streams of light that expanded to rivers of light, on whose shores many boats were kept tied up and ready. If I'm not mistaken, that tree there is hollow, I heard the reporter observe, and the best thing to do would be to shut that man inside the hollow tree trunk, that man meaning Kalkbrenner, whose desert story still hadn't come to an end, it won't do, said the reporter, to have Jacksch constantly interrupted. Then I saw Kalkbrenner's body being lowered down from the sky into the hollow tree trunk, he had already disappeared, but his head was still visible between the boughs, as if he had just been placed on top of the tree, and now the guests finally had him where most of them thought he belonged, he had difficulty breathing, he gasped, wheezed, and asked for something to drink, he whispered something about his being in imminent danger of drying out, we won't let you die of thirst, the male guests who had gathered around the tree called back to him, and while they kept saying, listen, we won't let you die of thirst, they opened their pants and urinated on the tree trunk.

Pay close attention, said the reporter, it's going to happen now, this is going to get interesting. He was right, because all of a sudden Jacksch grabbed the handle of the axe with both hands, yes, called the reporter enthusiastically, swing it!

Finally, Jacksch said, I grabbed the axe with both hands on the handle and raised it for the decisive blow, watch!

Yes, I saw Jacksch raising the axe for a terrible blow with the broad side, the axe with the cutting side up was already whizzing over his head, I saw the blade of the axe flash threateningly in the early sunlight breaking through the morning sky;

Listen, the axe, with the cutting side up, had already whizzed back over my head, Jacksch said to the party guests, and naturally I wanted to let the axe come whizzing down again immediately, broad side first, naturally, down on the head of the wedge and through the block at last, now or never, because it was really urgent that the piece of wood be split, you know—but it didn't happen.

Oh dear, said the reporter, that could have been avoided.

It didn't happen, said Jacksch, because behind my back the blade of the axe had gotten stuck somewhere, you know, behind me something must have gotten caught, you see, and of course I turned around right away, I wanted to know what was behind me.

Did you hear that sound just now, that muffled note that seemed to be sounding through felt? someone asked Pfeifer.

No, no, that was nothing, I don't want to hear anything about a note!

But there was one, it was like a sting intercepted by a thick felt covering, for instance, a sting into a firm pear . . .

Jacksch still had his fingers wrapped around the axe handle over his head when he turned around, it looked like the blade of his axe had gotten stuck in the air somewhere behind his back, so I turned around, said Jacksch, but I didn't see anything, he said, you see, there was really nothing to see, not a trace of the axe blade, and certainly no trace of what it might have gotten stuck in, he said, and there really was nothing to see, he kept shaking the axe handle over his head, I kept shaking it, he said, and finally I did get the blade free, explained Jacksch, breathing a sigh of relief, I breathed a sigh of relief, he said, it seemed that the worst was over, and naturally I wanted to carry out the decisive blow, he went on, but unfortunately it didn't work out that way.

I could have told you that, said the reporter.

I saw Jacksch preparing once again to smash the block of air in front of him to smithereens, but nothing came of it. Because suddenly it dawned on me, he explained, no, suddenly I saw the light, because suddenly I knew exactly where the axe blade had been stuck, the only place it could have been stuck back then, and I was deeply shocked.

What do you think, Jacksch asked the guests gathered around him, what do you think, where did the axe blade get stuck, you'll never guess, where was the only place it could have gotten stuck, what do you think, where?

Hey you, called the proctologist, turning away from the trunk of the tree to Jacksch, yes, you!

Me? asked Jacksch, lowering the axe.

Yes, you, please come over here, I think my eyes are playing tricks on me, said the proctologist, zipping up his pants.

Jacksch went over to him.

Please turn around! I think it was on the other side.

Jacksch turned around.

Yes, that's it, now what's this here?

What?

Don't you know what you have there?

How should I know? said Jacksch, not seeing anything.

Oh well, said the proctologist, you can't see it yourself, but to make up for that, I can see it all the more clearly. Now I think, on your, what do you call it, what's the word for that, yes, this place here, almost split, as I see, gaping open, quite right . . .

What?

Gaping open, I said, is the only correct way to describe it, tell me, does that happen often, of course it's not my area of specialty, but if need be . . .

What?

Well, this moist, gaping gash here on the back of your head, it's really strange . . .

You guessed it, Doctor, said Jacksch, the back of my head, the blade of the axe had gotten stuck in the back of my own head as I was raising my arms for the blow, and I realized it was urgent for me to do some very careful thinking about the state of my head!

You're quite right, answered the proctologist, it's a deep furrow-like fold, but it's clean and neatly done, I think it would be best for you if it were bandaged, just now it's starting to run a little, don't you feel that? but if you don't do something preventative, soon, then it'll drain you completely, do you understand, completely.

Come, said the hospital architect, right over there, a mere hundred meters away, is the nearest hospital that I've built, we'll all accompany you there, I'll show you the way, come along!

After the last group of people had pushed their way out through the garden gate and into the outskirts of the city, Johanna, her brother, Florian Waldstein, and I decided to make our way to the nearby little lake, since a cold little swim—we all felt a strong urge to feel the wind on our bare skin—was the best way to prepare for the coming loneliness. We went along the avenue of poplar trees that led from the outskirts of the city to the beach, its streetcar tracks covered with thick rust from a route that had been discontinued ages ago, and the black wooden cross-ties, screwed into the marshy soil, with birch saplings growing in the gravel between them, still gave out an intensely pungent smell of tar in the rising heat, and still didn't show any sign of rot in spite of the many decades of disuse, so that I couldn't help but secretly suspect that the cross-ties were still regularly serviced, even replaced, yes, the astoundingly black freshly gleaming surfaces of the ties led me to think that after the streetcar route had been discontinued, they had forgotten to cancel the track's cross-tie maintenance service, which had therefore continued to this very day.

The lake was surrounded by an extraordinarily wide ring of reeds.

It's often feared that some day this ring of reeds will close in on the water so tightly that the lake will dry up.

The bathing beach—which because of the reeds was unfortunately the only remaining open access to the water—was naturally closed at this early hour, so we climbed over the fence, which of course was forbidden.

In the middle of the bathing beach's sunbathing lawn there was a large, empty changing room: a stained black wooden shed several stories high that had a roof over it but was otherwise open to the air, the size of an average rental house, through whose individual stories thick wooden rods stretched from wall to wall about two meters up, sometimes lengthwise, sometimes crosswise, on which innumerable bare clothes hangers hung close together, clanking briskly in the morning wind.

Johanna and I wandered extensively through this large collection of empty coatracks, which, like the building itself, was already very old and historically significant, and was serviced regularly by the people who preserve historic monuments. In earlier times, all the inhabitants of the city are said to have washed their clothes in the lake water from time to time, or to have had them washed there by their servants, and afterwards hung them up to dry in this house full of hangers, in the same wind that still blows through the coatrack building today.

We were alone, the photographer and the painter were somewhere else.

From the top story we had a good view of the lake, a partially clouded mirror framed in green that stretched to the horizon, hanging itself up there by fastening itself to the sky with the ring of reeds on its opposite bank.

We undressed, I turned away from her rather bashfully (people still did that back then), and as I hung my clothes up on one of the hangers, I saw that she too, how should I put it, the wind had suddenly gotten surprisingly cool, yes, and perhaps that's why, all at once, we spontaneously embraced each other, no, I think a ring of air had forced our naked bodies toward each other, united them, closing firmly around us, yes, I had yearned for this in vain for so long, and now I was finally entwined in dreamlike real contact with Johanna's body.

All my sadness in my body flowed away from me and evaporated, and I felt the tube of air that was pushing us more and more closely together overlap both our heads, soft as stone; are you very cold, you're trembling, I asked her, but I saw that she wasn't trembling at all, but was quite calm, I wasn't feeling with my skin, but somehow with her skin, yes, it was with her smooth skin, clinging to her so persistently, that I was feeling my own trembling body;

no, I'm not cold, she replied, I feel myself trembling although I'm quite calm; and I see myself trembling, I said, but don't feel it in myself, only in you; probably, because I'm quite calm, I'm feeling your trembling body for you, she said, whereas you, because you're trembling all over, are feeling my perfectly calm body for me;

I'm trembling because I'm deeply moved, I replied, but you cushion the vibration of it in you, I hope you won't catch cold from all my trembling.

It's the trembling of excitement, not cold, said Johanna, come on, we'll exert ourselves in order to relax one another, I'll tell you listening *very deeply* to myself, *what* you're feeling, *and* you'll sink yourself entirely into yourself *and describe to me* what I'm experiencing.

Yes, it's a well-balanced agitation; yes, there's a hint of kind but confident anxiety; all in all it's a pleasingly calming excitement, it moves me in a relaxed way, very precisely blurred;

Yes, I feel myself completely relaxed, almost to the breaking point, and also somehow kneaded and caressed.

Lying close together we had really exchanged our senses, for a while I could experience my own existence only with and through Johanna's consciousness, so deeply had we already dreamed our way into each other, in such a hurried respite, culminating in such a mild frenzy,

more and more we were both overcome by a profound but loving agony, making us blissfully happy, and we thought that a heated liquid had been poured over us, boiling hot though cooled to the freezing point.

Exhausted, we lay sticking to each other under the roof of the changing-room building and were seized by a liberating, quite nostalgic wanderlust, it was a longing for foreign lands that were entirely unknown to us, where we had never been, but where we would nevertheless always be right at home.

We got up. I buried my head in her long hair, through which, veiled in yellow, I first saw the smoke-filled morning silhouette of the hungover outskirts of the city, but then very fleetingly also discerned the outline of Florian Waldstein, probably, who, when he saw us, turned away in shock, and stumbled down the wooden stairs.

Then I heard footsteps down below moving away through the grass to the beach.

On the shore, the painter's clothing was organized in a bundle on the sand; he had swum out ahead of us. We too wanted to wash away the party, but instead we just took a quick dip and went freezing back to the changing-room building, got dressed again and returned to the beach, to await Waldstein.

We watched silently for a long time, squatting in the morning wind that was blowing on us from the lake and plucking the steel cables that ran along the masts of the unrigged sailboats anchored nearby. With fixed concentration, we watched the surface of the water, fringed and framed by reeds, searching for the painter's head gliding over them, coming back towards us.

Maybe he's just being obscured by the ruffled mist over the water, so that we can't see him, I said, and Diabelli, also waiting on the beach, remembered that at the same time last year we had also had to wait over half an hour for Waldstein to come back. The bathing beach opens at eight o'clock. Since we wanted to avoid having the beach attendants, who'd be showing up soon, arrest, detain, and prosecute us as vagrants, burglars, thieves, or, anyway, trespassers—and that much we could hardly deny—we had to go back out over the fence as quickly and unobtrusively as possible.

Since we didn't want to leave the painter behind by himself, however, immediately after we left the beach, just in the nick of time, by climbing the fence, we went back via the main entrance, which had just opened, as the first paying guests of the day, in order to wait serenely for Waldstein to return and to stand by him during the difficulties he would presumably be experiencing with the beach authorities soon, if they happened to figure out that he'd visited the city's recreational site outside of business hours.

But to our surprise his clothing was still lying as before on the same part of the beach, and we continued waiting for him for most of that early morning, though naturally as time passed our concern about his increasingly puzzling whereabouts became outright fear, while we watched the beach workers go about their monotonous work.

They were busy making the long docks that reached more than two hundred meters out onto the surface of the lake usable for the swimmers who were gradually filling the beach by laying out the boards that they had taken up from the frames of the docks the previous evening and stored overnight. The lifeguard who was supervising these workers obviously took us for foreigners, to whom the local routines were incomprehensible, and therefore had to be explained. The boards from the docks have to be taken up from the frames every evening, he said, stored in a sheltered place overnight, and then put back every morning, in order to protect the boards—which on account of the prevailing shortage of wood everywhere in the country represent no small investment—first of all from the rain, so that they last longer, and second of all in order to forestall their otherwise inevitable theft.

Because if the boards were to remain on the docks overnight, the lifeguard went on, then they would be taken down and stolen, both behind our backs and in front of our eyes, so quickly we wouldn't have time to introduce any countermeasures, since we would be up against the superior might of the majority of the population, because if it got out that the boards were left on the bathing docks for even a single night, the news would be everywhere in no time at all. Given the catastrophic lack of fuel in this area and the resulting price of wood, you can't blame people. It's perfectly normal in the summer for people to start procuring firewood for the coming winter, but in the last few years it's become the habit for most people to actually start pre-heating their homes for the coming winter while it's still the middle of summer outside.

In fact, he told us, several years ago—as though we all weren't already quite aware—in the middle of the summer, it had suddenly become unexpectedly cold in the city, and it had even begun to snow, so people were naturally utterly helpless, confronted with a cold the likes of which they'd never even experienced in winter. The district heating plants were of course snowed in, they became iced-over and couldn't be started, and people had neither enough proper stoves nor adequate firewood or other fuel at their disposal; admittedly, the lifeguard had been able to get hold of what was probably enough firewood for the members of his own family, as you can imagine, he told us, pointing and winking at the bathing dock boards, but it proved impossible for him to find a proper stove anywhere.

That sudden, terrible cold several years ago, right in the middle of the summer, caused many people to take preventive measures for the future, he said, so that they would never again be helpless in the face of that kind of cold: now they simply can't be dissuaded from keeping the heat on as much as possible, *above all in the summer*, especially in the hottest months, year by year as the summer gets hotter they are increasingly fearful that a sudden catastrophic cold as severe or even worse will return at any second, and so they heat their homes most right in the hottest midsummer months, and the hotter the summer, the more actively certain segments of the population heat their homes, said the lifeguard.

On the way to the Beach Police Office, a wooden shed built half on land and half in the water, the lifeguard continued talking about the origins of the fuel shortage and the unbelievable price of firewood, soon everything in our country that's even slightly combustible will vanish, he said, would be burned away as fuel.

Two hours, said the inspector behind his desk in the Beach Police Office, shaking his head, that's no good, you must be mistaken, because two hours ago neither you nor your missing acquaintance could have been here, you couldn't have gotten in, because two hours ago everything here was still locked up.

Asking us to rethink the statements that we'd just made, so that the proper measures could be taken, the inspector attempted to encourage us in our reflections by saying: perhaps in all your quite understandable excitement concerning the worrisome absence of your acquaintance—who may have just swum out two minutes ago—you've become so bewildered that two minutes' time seems as long to you as two hours.

No, Diabelli replied, we climbed over the fence much longer than two hours ago, when the beach was still closed, and that was when Waldstein swam out into the lake.

No sooner had Diabelli spoken the words "climbed over the fence" than the inspector awoke with a jerk from his initial lethargy, over the fence, he said, over the fence, of course that changes everything completely, he spoke now of an entirely new starting position, of aspects previously and unfortunately not taken into consideration, and said that it was high time to pursue this matter with a precise and thorough investigation.

He still hasn't come back yet? he asked, how can you be so sure of that?

His clothes, answered Diabelli, they're still lying on the beach.

Getting up from his desk, the inspector ordered the lifeguard to send out the rescue and diving teams.

Only now did I see that the rear of the office led directly into a boathouse; out of the darkness of the boathouse roof truss, the boats that had been concealed up there were now being swung down, already manned by figures holding all kinds of equipment, onto the surface of the water, darkened by the shadow of the inspector's desk,

our lifeboats, too, whispered the lifeguard, have to be stored away at night so that no one can find them, because otherwise they too would inevitably be used for fuel.

Sitting inside the wide boathouse, where we were detained for several hours, the entire building seemed to me like a huge *official jellyfish balloon* anchored on the shore of the sky, acting mechanically and automatically administering the surrounding countryside, letting the various boats down from its pointed doorways onto the water, dispersing them widely over the whole surface of the lake, which I could almost see in its entirety as I watched the vessels gliding out through the police doors, yes, from the office to the opposite horizon the entire surface of the water was evenly covered with small boats whose tentacles systematically searched every square on their map, so that in time every cubic centimeter of the liquid landscape was sieved through at least once during the investigation, which was watched by the inspector with interest as he spat out into the water from his desk covered with papers.

We can hardly allow the bathers, he said, to swim in a recreational lake that has a rotting corpse drifting around on the bottom.

Suddenly all the people in the inspector's office stood up and the inspector bowed toward the door, through which a higher official arrived, presumably everyone's superior, a man who was greeted and subsequently addressed by the inspector as "Commissioner," and who casually commented to the inspector that it was excellent to have notified him without delay, he went to the inspector's place behind the desk, sat down, and began to leaf through a file he'd brought along with a look expressing the greatest concentration.

What has the search turned up so far? he asked.

Fearing the devastating consequences of his answer, the lifeguard replied: nothing found, not a trace, simply gone.

Then the Commissioner, continuing to leaf through the file, wanted to know if not even a corpse had been found, saying that a human body can't simply dissolve in water, asking whether they had done a proper enough search.

Combed every centimeter, was the hesitant answer: on the bottom of the lake and also in the reeds, practically with a magnifying glass. We only have the clothes, which were of course immediately impounded.

His worst suspicions seemed in every respect to be proving well-founded, responded the Commissioner, turning toward us:

Your acquaintance has already been under suspicion for quite a long time, we had considered detaining him many times before, only the last conclusive pieces of evidence were missing, and they have now been furnished at last. His disappearing without a trace, such a thing is—as you know—not possible, and when that sort of thing happens there's always something that isn't right, which something can however be unambiguously explained in this particular case:

This painter—probably his so-called artistic calling was in any case just a clever way of disguising his opposition to the basic order of our city—was nothing other than a *spy*, yes, indeed, an agent, who, after he got wind of something unexpected, something unpredictable, after things had become too hot for him here, was probably taken up, without anyone having noticed, was probably picked up by a seaplane that he'd arranged to have land on the lake early this morning, and in fact presumably stark naked or at best in swimming trunks, and he probably deliberately left his clothes behind to give the false impression that he had drowned.

Since you, not only through your suspicious and to us very questionable acquaintance with this gentleman, but additionally through your illegal presence on the beach during his disappearance, are very much involved in this case, more so than can be comfortable

—you will in any case still have to answer to the appropriate district courts for your knowingly committed trespass, a fact you freely admitted when in full possession of your mental faculties—,

I will unfortunately have to oblige you to be available to me at all times. I probably don't need to mention that you are of course forbidden to leave the city without first requesting that your departure be authorized by the police, and I of course will see to it that such a request will not be granted, even in the most urgent of circumstances.

Good day.

It was already afternoon when we returned exhausted to the garden, where the servant and his helpers were clearing up.

The landscape was exhausted, beaten up by the sky of this day—the hills paralyzed, the mountain behind them propped up on crutches as if just about to crumble.

The trees and bushes in the garden had fallen asleep, with the old hollow tree snoring particularly loudly and now also belching into the clouds above it, and these and other very untreelike noises it was making were due to the fact that people had forgotten Kalkbrenner, who was still lodged in the hollow trunk, we wanted to get him out right away, but the poet was still sleeping, we woke him, then with our help he crept out of his plant prison all squashed and went staggering away.

Wait, I called after him and asked him please, whenever it was convenient, to give me the exact wording of his story about the music that he had read aloud at the end of the previous night, I would like to set it to music, I explained, to write music for his story about music.

But he didn't know anything about it, what music? he asked, what kind of story am I supposed to have written?

He turned away, shaking his head uncomprehendingly, went out the gate, and became smaller in the sweltering landscape.

All the photos that Diabelli had taken of the party were piled up on one of the tables, and with more disgust than happy memories, I began to study them.

There I saw again the two photos of me beside the statue by the pond, bringing to mind the circumstances of how the second one was shot, the second photograph being basically identical to and interchangeable with the first, which was, however, a year older.

Then I saw a picture of Kalkbrenner demonstrating his sucking-gullet phenomenon, and there were two of that one as well, also doubles of the town planner drawing a circle on the table in front of him, likewise twin photos of Waldstein and me in the wicker chairs carrying on our conversation with our eyes closed, and then naturally two identical photos of the helpless Schleifer standing in front of the locked piano and simply not being able to open it, and then, among others, two exactly the same of the firmly belted pianist playing forcefully at the keyboard, two of Kalkbrenner suspended in the air, and then further twofold documentations of our wandering along the avenue of poplars to the shore of the lake, and of us at the bathing beach in the dressing-room building, and then also on the beach itself . . .

Why were all the photos *twofold and identical?*

I was about to ask the photographer what fancy technical gadget he had on his camera that caused every shot to be *exposed twice simultaneously*, when it occurred to me that in each case one of the twin photographs was from the party last year and the second from the party this year, they were as good as identical with each other, alike as two peas in a pod, indistinguishable.

I began setting up a chronologically systematic order to the photos, which I laid out on the table in rows of two, like playing cards.

I asked Diabelli which of the identical photos were from the party this year and which from the party last year.

After he had spent a while assessing with expert eyes the rows I had laid out in optical pairs, he answered that it was impossible to determine that sort of thing now, because the pictures are too alike; then he spoke of his regrettable carelessness, recklessly and to his chagrin letting the photos get mixed up, and not having kept them separate from the start, he wouldn't let that happen in future, but now no other more favorable systematic order could be brought to them beyond the one that I had just set up, for which he thanked me, by the way.

Didn't it make him happy at all that the REPETITION OF THE PARTY that he had talked about continually yesterday afternoon had without a doubt been an unambiguous success, as proven by these paired pieces of photographic evidence—or hadn't that occurred to him yet?

Or had he and his sister long since forgotten about their plan, or suppressed their knowledge of it?

I didn't necessarily want to be the first person to bring it up, the two of them might think I was completely crazy. Or they'll suddenly deny everything, I thought.

So I had probably told Johanna last year too, in exactly the same way, the story about my vanished girlfriend, and I was particularly shocked to discover that there were also two identical photographs showing me lying with Johanna under the roof of the top story of the changing-room building, I wondered what consequences that would have both for the relationship we began last year as well as for the relationship we'd begun today, I would have liked to make those photos disappear immediately, but even that probably wouldn't change anything, I thought.

So it had turned out to be exactly the same party as last year, right down to the smallest details: much as I could no longer tell which photos were from last year's party and which were from the party this year, it was exactly the same now with the pictures surfacing in my memory: when I thought of moments or events from the the party last year or the party this year, I couldn't tell the pictures apart, they were also turning up in twos in my head, absolutely identical silhouettes and chains of associations from both events: when I thought over my worries about the party, I no longer had even the faintest idea whether I was worrying about this year's party or last year's: as though, in my head, *both parties had been identi-*

cally depicted, each on its own transparent film and then laid over one another with all the elements coinciding . . .

Indeed, until a certain point, everything yesterday and today had been exactly the same as last year—there was no other way to explain it. Up to the disappearance of the painter Florian Waldstein, that is, who still hasn't reappeared. Yes, last year too we had waited out there at the lake for the painter, but last year he had come back again after half an hour.

Waldstein's disappearance without a trace was the first thing today that had *not* been the same as last year,

it's possible that this was necessary, necessary for us to break free from the captivity of yesterday's last year or last year's yesterday. Otherwise it's possible that everything else would have proceeded and progressed as it had last year and been repeated over and over again.

Presumably, then, everything that followed would have gone on as well, winding up and winding down exactly as it had last year, until finally sliding into yet another repetition of the party, a repetition of the repetition of the party, whereupon yet again everything would have progressed as it had the previous year, in order to flow then into yet another repetition of the party, a repetition of the repetition of the repetition of last year's party.

And everything else would for all time have abruptly and unalterably again and again been exactly as it was last year.

Time would have gotten caught in an endless loop—everything always for all time would just have circled around itself.

And not only we but everyone else as well would never again have had an opportunity to improve or even alter the intolerable circumstances and unreasonable, adverse conditions of our environment. We would never have been able to accomplish anything at all.

Probably the painter's disappearing without a trace was also the first thing that enabled us to reestablish a critical distance from our own memories, since during yesterday's party none of the participants had been aware of the ongoing repetition for even a moment.

Waldstein had already realized all this, probably much earlier than me, I thought, and because he refused to submit to this eternal recurrence, he just left, as inconspicuously as possible . . .

In the garden his paintings which exactly recreated individual segments of the garden were were still hanging on the trees.

What are you talking about? asked Diabelli, presumably I had been thinking out loud. I was thinking about the repetition of the party, I replied.

What? asked Diabelli, and said he didn't understand what I was getting at. Do you know what he's talking about? he asked his sister.

No, answered Johanna, a repetition? What kind of repetition? And all your careful planning, I said.

Planning, said Johanna, what kind of planning? The planning of a repetition? The planning of a repetition of what? And when are we supposed to have talked about these plans?

Yesterday afternoon, I said, don't you remember, I wanted to leave, to have nothing to do with it, but you knew how to keep me here.

What are we actually supposed to have planned to repeat? asked Johanna. Are you saying that the party we've just thrown was similar to the party we threw last year? But she didn't think so at all, quite the opposite; if nothing else, the sad incident of Florian Waldstein's disappearance was more than enough to make this year's party fundamentally different from all other previous parties, or so she thought . . .

Her self-confidence provoked me, so I let myself get carried away and showed her the pair of photos that I'd wanted at first to destroy, those pictures that showed our intimate embrace in the changing-room building by the lake; here, I said, see, this one is after the party last year, and here, this is this morning . . .

What are you trying to get at? asked Johanna excitedly, if it upsets you so, she said, in the future she would see that that sort of thing would by no means be repeated . . .

Last year, said Diabelli, what happened last year? If I'm not mistaken, there wasn't a party at all last year. Was there?

Right you are, said Johanna, last year there was nothing, we didn't do anything at all, there was no party.

And the photos here, I exclaimed.

The photos, said Diabelli, they're from the party two years ago, no, even earlier, from the party three years ago.

But that can't be, I said, because as far as I'm concerned, I wasn't at any party two years ago, and not three years ago either—I was here for the first time last year.

Diabelli didn't know anything more about last year, all gone, as good as extinguished.

His sister had no memory of it either.

That's because your memory of last year's party coincides so closely with your memory of last night, I said.

Why? asked Johanna.

Because it's possible that last night and the party a year ago were entirely identical, I explained, as though last night was already a whole year old, or last year's party only happened last night.

Shortly after this I was standing with Diabelli in the far third of the garden on the shore of the little pond in front of the moss-covered sandstone statue; I took the two identical photos in which I was standing beside the sandstone statue, looking at the grass with an uncertain, searching expression, and showed these to him.

Late yesterday afternoon, I said, we were standing rather like we are now, but at first only one of the two photos existed, didn't it?

The photographer nodded.

Then it occurred to me, I went on to explain, that something wasn't right, something to do with the statue's head: in the one-year-old party photo, here, one of the two, the statue was headless, but the statue standing there both yesterday and now today definitely has a head on it, and yesterday I wanted to draw your attention most emphatically to this—in my opinion, decisive—difference, to show you what was, in my opinion, a crucial oversight, yes?

The photographer nodded.

But it wasn't easy to make you understand what was to me a clear statement of fact, I went on to say, it all seemed too sudden for you, so I was forced to demonstrate it. I took the headless statue photo here, and said to you, do you see, in the photo from last year this statue is headless, then I stepped closer to the statue, in order to point out to you most emphatically the fact that its head was intact, and so, you see, I called out to you, your statue which is obviously headless in the photo has its head quite clearly mounted on it here and now, and in order finally to demonstrate this reality to you incontrovertibly, I wanted to show you just how firmly the stone head was attached to the statue's body, but I'd hardly brushed it when it suddenly fell off, broke away, and fell into the grass, whereupon I looked helplessly after it, searching for it, and in that very moment you took the picture, that's how the second photo came into being, the second one that can't be distinguished from the first, and then you were finally able to prove to *me* what you had been wanting to then for a long time . . .

No, Diabelli interrupted me, I didn't want to prove anything! All I did was take a picture! Nothing more! What was I supposed to have proved to you? There was nothing to prove!

So you want to dispute everything again and reject it? I said to the photographer. But you can't deny it anymore now! I was standing here yesterday, holding the headless statue photo in one hand, and with my other hand reaching for the statue—and now you don't want to admit any of it—whereupon the head fell off, that's exactly how it was, look here, I reached for the stone head exactly like so, pay close attention:

(I grabbed at the nymph's stony curls several times, but this had no effect whatsoever—probably it's somewhat more firmly attached today than yesterday, I thought, and resorted to more violent measures, tried forcibly to push the head down from the body, but it just didn't want to fall, even though I began to shake the goddess's head with all my strength).

Why won't her head fall off? I called out, desperate with rage, while Diabelli alternately examined one of the headless statue photos and evaluated my efforts to tear off the head in front of him;

the head should have fallen off already, I called.

It's *firmly* attached, said Diabelli, very firmly.

Among the pairs of photos that I had assembled there were some that were no longer entirely alike. Two of them, for example, now differed in the following way:

in the first photo Johanna, the painter Florian Waldstein, and I were all standing in front of Waldstein's painting hanging under the hollow tree, the surface of the painting obscuring the view toward the garden gate, and on which this particular obscured garden gate was portrayed; the painter was standing in front of the garden gate he had painted as though he wanted to take hold of

the two-dimensional door handle on the gate; in the second photo
of this set, however, only Johanna and I are still standing in front
of the painting, looking into the picture as though *watching* the
painter Florian Waldstein who had by now *gone into his picture*, having just walked through the garden gate he had painted and closed
it behind him, and while Johanna was receiving many telephone
calls of thanks, in which people were assuring her of the unsur-
passable *uniqueness* of the party, we could hear the announcer on
a radio that was playing somewhere saying we would now hear a
new, previously unknown poem by Kalkbrenner:

> *Slavery*
> *is abolished*
> *by tyrants*
> *injustice*
> *is done away with*
> *by oppressors*
> *prisoners*
> *are freed*
> *by slave-traders*
> *the tortured*
> *are comforted*
> *by torturers*
> *the truth*
> *is proclaimed*
> *by notorious liars*
> *and closely guarded secrets*
> *are kept under lock and key*
> *by discreet traitors*

GRADUS AD PARNASSUM

If you compare a house, or a building, with a person, or a person's head, I said to my brother some time later, then the attic is the brain of the building.

For years, much more than a decade, in fact almost twenty years, my brother and I had studied music at the Conservatory, especially piano, and in the course of our time there had gotten to know and had used almost every room in the building, but never had the opportunity to go into the attic; the brain of the institute had always been kept from us, and it was only after we had already been away from our studies for more than decade that we were compelled, by chance, as it happens, to look into that brain, during a vain attempt to visit our old piano teacher.

It's a considerable achievement, my brother said when we were standing outside Hellberger's studio, that we've found our teacher's studio again right away, without any searching around, without any difficulty, immediately, that is, as though we had last been there only yesterday. Of course I'd been afraid at first that we wouldn't be able to find the right studio after so many years, my brother had

had quite a time persuading me to go into the institute at all, and owing to my physical, but above all emotional, condition, I was anxious and uncertain—just come, he said, it'll do you good, he pulled me through the entrance hall up over the flights of stairs, and then in no time at all we were standing outside Hellberger's studio.

Of course we only succeeded in finding it, my brother explained, because our teacher has always taught in the same room, has taught there for decades now, ever since he became a member of the institute, quite unlike his colleagues who were always changing or exchanging their studios: several times a week, in extreme cases, but at least once a semester. Even back then, when we were studying with him, our teacher was always telling us how he hated this constant exchanging of studios, in this regard he did *not* understand his colleagues at all, and as far as he was concerned, he was not going to be one of those regular studio changers, let alone one of those regular studio exchangers.

My brother knocked, no answer, the studio door was locked, no one there, what a pity, we come back again after so many years, said my brother, and there's no one in.

In the corridor the elevator door happened to be open, my brother pulled me in, then we rode slowly upward into the roof truss. There are well over a hundred pianos stored in the attic of the institute, my brother was filled with enthusiasm, he wouldn't have thought the Conservatory had such a spacious superstructure, he rhapsodized over this superb store of valuable instruments all in a single room, saying that one seldom had the opportunity in life to see this sort of thing in person, he spoke of a mounting interest that was lately spreading to all levels of society, an interest in the most profound productions, musical ones in particular, of course, it was admirable how people were increasingly keen on artistic training, musical training in particular, of course, an essential component of education again, and all along the line it could be observed that with the cultivation of art, music in particular, of course, comes the fulfillment of a deep inner need. My brother took out the tuning hammer that he always carries with him, opened several pianos, examined them, tried to tune them, looked up in astonishment, and soon I saw him pacing nervously back and forth, finding fault with the rather inadequate conditions in which the pianos were stored there, the skylights that were possibly open day and night resulting in a constant draught, the not only unfeeling but also grossly negligent treatment of the pianos, he started swearing, whereupon from one of the instruments startled doves came fluttering out that had obviously been nesting there, the dust, cried my brother, the dust in the felts, do you see, the moths, he reached into one of the pianos with his right hand and brought out a handful of dirt, here, he called to me, a handful of dirt from the surface of a single octave, and with a thorough cleaning you'd be forced to take whole pails and buckets of filth from a single grand piano, shocking! screamed my brother, it's shocking how an institute, indeed, a conservatory that is dedicated exclusively to music and musical instruments treats the instruments it is so fortunate to have at its disposal!

I watched my brother waving his tuning hammer around threateningly, opening a few more of the instruments, closing them again, looking into the matter more closely, then I heard him breathe a sigh of relief, yes, he said, that's the solution, there's no other way I could explain this to myself, these pianos are worn out from decades of lessons, no longer usable, and repairs are no longer justifiable, repair costs have risen so high recently that especially complicated repairs are hardly cost-effective, since the price of these repairs is as a rule only insignificantly lower than the cost of a new piano, usually identical with the cost of a new piano, in fact, and there are also cases, said my brother, where the cost of repairs significantly exceeds the cost of buying a new instrument. Nothing but ruined receptacles for classical music in the Conservatory, where conditions get worse every year, I allowed myself to remark, whereupon my brother immediately referred me back to my own condition, from one detox phase to another your own condition is getting worse, and so you're projecting your predicament onto your environment, which is completely unwarranted of course, he said, you can't draw conclusions about your environment based solely on yourself, where else should they store the pianos that aren't good for lessons anymore but here, it's the obvious solution.

In the brain of the building, I thought, in every brain there's an accumulation of junk, because everything that you yourself have destroyed or that someone else has destroyed for you is stored in the brain where it takes up an amazing amount of space and distorts this space until your head is so full of it that it bursts like a balloon you bought at the fair.

Whenever I walk through the city or the surrounding countryside, I often hear a curious cracking and popping, as if balloons were bursting around me all the time, I keep a look-out for balloons floating overhead, but there are none to be seen. Probably the cracking and popping is just some people's heads about to burst, the sounds are distorted by the air, carried farther, ultimately it's a matter of how long the people are able to hold their heads together by force. If you were to examine the air around you more closely, you'd notice the many head particles, head fragments floating away over the villages, and think how much head dust is blown through the countryside by the winds.

We're going, said my brother, we're leaving right away, an environment like this is no good for your present condition.

In the meantime, the elevator we had come up on had gone back down again without us, my brother wanted to summon it again, he was looking for a certain button, where's the button here, I heard him asking, there has to be a button here somewhere that we can press to bring the elevator back up again, but I don't see the so-called call-button.

We'll have to go down on foot, he said, take the stairs, the stairwell, the entire building has stairwells running through it.

While my brother went looking for the stairs, my head was filled with stairwells, for the most part they're completely empty, I thought, because people use the elevators, if you wander up or down a stairwell, you find complete solitude there, stairwells are usually the only places where you can think undisturbed about the conditions in the buildings that house them, and if you wander up or down a stairwell, the only people you meet are also thoughtfully wandering up or down the stairwell, or are sitting or lying in the stairwells pursuing some highly intellectual activity, they are people for whom the silence of the stairwells has become a vital necessity . . . It's hardly conceivable, I heard my brother say, getting worried, that there's no staircase here, the building code for all buildings requires that all stories including the attic be joined by stairwells, but possibly the stairs leading down from the attic are dangerous or defective, so they've been boarded up or closed off.

Of course even in defective stairwells, I thought, you can find highly intellectual people who very often overlook the fact that they're sitting in a defective stairwell, the staircases are often defective and unsafe particularly in those buildings where people engage in the highest intellectual pursuits not only in the stairwells, but also in the other rooms, especially there, I thought, many highly intellectually active people who live in the stairwells fall down the systems of steps there, the systems that are collapsing in on themselves, and are buried alive . . .

I heard my brother nervously drumming on the elevator door with his fists, shouting down, can't anyone hear anything, doesn't anybody hear me!

Now to make matters worse a fleet of elevators were also boring their way into my brain, the elevators with which the people who use elevators reach the rooms where they have to perform the various tasks that they think are to their own advantage, yes, they despise and deride the people who live in the stairwells, I thought, they make fun of them publicly, even though the people who live in stairwells are not only thinking about and working on their own stairwell problems, but also and above all on the difficulties of the people who are busy in the other rooms, they try to draw these people's attention to their unfortunate situation by bluffing their way into the elevators and other rooms in the building in order to study the intolerable conditions there, but then they're usually found out because of their defiant way of speaking and their all-too-conspicuous behavior, people laugh at them and send them back to the stairwells . . .

My brother had given up his vain attempts to call attention to us, it's embarrassing, he said, this situation we've gotten ourselves into, we'll have to wait for the caretaker, the caretaker may take the elevator up soon, caretakers often have things to do in their attics several times a day, said my brother, I'm sure the caretaker of this building is required to inspect all the rooms of the building from the basement to the attic several times a day, so that he can inform the director at any time of the condition of all the rooms including the attic, to keep the director adequately informed about the conditions of the various Conservatory holdings, so that the director in turn is in a position to report to his superiors in the government at any time the condition in which the Conservatory finds itself.

Getting back to me, my brother said, your condition is alarming, especially in this environment, and now especially in this situation, you have to be patient, he said, it can't last long, do you have the pills the doctor prescribed for your depression with you? Of course I had them with me, but there wasn't a glass of water anywhere and my mouth was completely dried out, and not only my hands were trembling, but my entire body as well.

Naturally the withdrawal symptoms get progressively worse the more often you allow yourself these excesses of yours, said my brother, that go on for days—when you go on one of your binges sometimes you're continually drunk for over a week, you drink until you pass out or simply fall down, and as soon as you're up again the first thing you do is reach for the bottle. And when you can't get your hands on any alcohol at home, because all the alcohol is being kept away from you, is being kept under lock and key, you leave the house under the pretext of having to buy yourself a certain newspaper, book, or musical score, right away, just so that you can start drinking again in the nearest pub, my brother said, after which you stock up at a shop with as many hip-flasks as you can easily hide, and then you continue drinking secretly at home until you fall down or pass out again, until in the normal course of these kind of days your body begins to defend itself so vituperatively against such treatment that you become unable to leave the house.

My brother is right.

The withdrawal symptoms were worse than ever. The constant nausea, the trembling, not only in my fingers, but in my entire body, the sweating, the back pains, the impaired balance, the fear of collapsing in the middle of the street—when we had been walking along the lakeshore on the way to the Conservatory, the trees had suddenly begun to move by themselves in the still, motionless air, without any wind, and then the thin branches of the weeping willow that were hanging down to the surface of the water caught hold of me with their tentacles, pulled me up, up into the clouds and then threw me back down into the lake!

You describe yourself as a so-called "periodic drunk," said my brother, and of course you don't forget to mention that once, for a full two years, you were drunk not just once every three months, but every single day. So you have "worked your way up" from being a chronic alcoholic to being a periodic drunk. Unfortunately, however, you aren't only getting drunk every three months, as you insist, but at least once a month, usually every two weeks, in fact. The intervals of time between your binges are getting shorter and shorter again. It would be better for you if you weren't endowed with that disastrous talent of yours. Up to eighty percent of writers, painters, and composers like you are chronic alcoholics or periodic drunks. Less so the orchestral musicians, because the nature of their profession doesn't really allow for such excesses. Whereas pianists or violinists are seldom drunk when they play public concerts, you're pretty much always drunk when you conduct one of your compositions or play it on the piano at a public concert, giving the impression that even you can't bear the sound of your work when you're sober.

The elevator motor started up, see now, said my brother, maybe the caretaker's coming already, but the caretaker didn't come, the late afternoon sun poured in through the skylights, be patient, said my brother, just be patient a little longer, the caretaker is probably inspecting the lower levels right now and will be up in the next few minutes.

I didn't want to come, I said to my brother reproachfully, if it had been up to me, we would have been spared all this, but you forced me both into the Conservatory and up here into the attic.

You should be thankful, my brother replied, I wanted to help cheer you up, a visit with Hellberger! Where would you be today if I didn't look after you?

Certainly not up here in the attic, I replied.

You're ungrateful, replied my brother bitterly, of course I too could have become an accomplished pianist, but unfortunately I have the most unfavorably constituted hands imaginable, particularly my fourth finger, which is always a terrible problem for pianists, I would have had to practice systematically at least eleven hours a day every day in order to be able to move my fourth finger independently of my third or even my fifth finger, and it's this ability that ensures that you can play a scale or an arpeggio exactly evenly in every respect, especially as far as the quality of touch on each individual note, I was lacking neither the stamina nor the diligence, particularly with regard to the latter I have always been well equipped, especially compared to you, but I was lacking the necessary time, since in order to attain that level of skill I would have had to devote myself exclusively to playing the piano, neglecting all my other studies, which would have made me develop into a completely one-sided person, like you yourself have become.

With regard to that, I said, you imitated Robert Schumann. No, replied my brother vehemently, I didn't imitate him, I constructed a different apparatus for myself that was entirely my own, not only differing from the Schumann construction but eliminating all its drawbacks.

I remember that before we took our final examinations in music my brother had screwed a completely useless gadget around his fingers and soon after maintained that he couldn't move his fingers at all anymore.

Just as Robert Schumann only became a composer when he could no longer move his fourth finger, my brother explained, I only became a piano mover when I couldn't move any of my fingers anymore. But then one day you started drinking like crazy, I think it was when one of your girlfriends went missing without a trace, something like that, anyway, at first no one thought much about it, sometimes a composer has to live it up and let himself go in order to recover from all his sensitive musical inventions, and people showed you a certain understanding. You had your first successes behind you, and the premiere of your FIVE BIG PIECES FOR ORCHESTRA, opus 5, was rapidly approaching. People hoped that this premiere would be well reviewed, and not only in specialist publications, said my brother—and it actually was—and that this would help you regain the necessary self-confidence you'd lost. But at the premiere you were drunker than you'd been in a long time, and in your terrible condition, in the bar after the concert, you swore at and insulted first the conductor, then the concert master, and then even your publisher, to whom you owe everything, which hurt you considerably, because after that the concert organizers, conductors, and practicing musicians, as well as your publisher, quite rightly became more cautious around you. Since then you've neither scored any other successes worth mentioning nor composed anything worth mentioning that comes anywhere close to the quality of your Pieces for Orchestra, with the exception of your opera with the oh-so-original title of "Opera," on which—with the greatest effort—you used up the last of your strength; naturally you offered the work to all the better opera houses, said my brother, but all the artistic directors who thought very highly of the work and wrote intelligent feature articles, scholarly articles, and observations about it were incapable of accepting the work for performance, impossible to perform, simply impossible to perform! In that opera you portrayed both the impossibility of opera generally as well as the impossibility of your own opera specifically, it's impossible to stage it, it's through-composed, and staging that sort of thing presents numerous insurmountable difficulties for traditional opera folk and is therefore impossible, your oversensitivity, in other words, has turned into a lack of respect directed against you yourself and your own art, and the only thing that can possibly help you now, said my brother, is a regular, proper job that distracts you from yourself, so that you don't destroy yourself once and for all!

Back when they offered you the position of second conductor in Linz, you shouldn't have been allowed to turn it down, you should have been forced to accept it! But even I would be happy to help you; I've frequently offered you a proper, regular job in piano moving. As you know, after successfully completing my degree in music, I took several courses lasting several years at the local Institute for the Promotion of the Economy, and following that, with great effort and industry, I built up my piano-moving business, with the help of which—not only in this city or this country, but in the whole world—I can always move enough pianos from somewhere to somewhere into somewhere out of somewhere in any case around somewhere and make myself a decent living! A little experience in piano moving would be of the greatest benefit not only to you, said my brother, but also to all other composers as well!

Once you've adequately studied the road and the distance you need to cover in transporting a piano, you can devote the utmost attention to the appropriate packaging! In a corner of the attic, my brother found a large case usually used for shipping grand pianos and corresponding exactly in its shape to a grand piano that has had its legs unscrewed.

No composer today should be allowed to compose a single note, said my brother, without proven experience in the piano-shipping business! Of course the shipping case has to be made a little larger than the piano; the piano has to have a little room to move in its case! The distance between the outer edges of the piano and the inner walls and paneling of its case has to be at least three, but preferably five centimeters. That leaves enough space around the edges of the piano for it to breathe, which is of the greatest importance, but of course it has to be firmly fastened in the corners to prevent it from rattling around in the case during transport over what are often the worst streets and roads. The case consists, as you can see, of an outer wall, usually of oak, and an inner wall, which is made up of paneling in softwood, usually pine, and indeed the inner paneling needs to be of pine because the softwood allows the wood on the outer edges of the piano to breathe naturally; it also allows for a so-called hygroscopicity, a certain retention of moisture that corresponds exactly to the normal room conditions the piano has come from and comes as close as possible to reflecting the natural state of the instrument; it also serves to increase the elasticity of the case. Not to forget that between the outer case wall and the inner case paneling as well as partly between the inner case paneling and the outer wood of the piano there must absolutely in all instances be enough eelgrass and tow to provide a slightly elastic but stationary, so-called stable resistance. For the construction of less expensive cases, the outer case walls can also, if you like, be made of white beech or common beech or copper beech instead of expensive oak, said my brother. For reasons of security it's advisable to add extra screws or nails to the outer walls of the case at those places that are particularly under stress during transport, or best of all to add *both* screws and nails. The customer who doesn't consider any of these precautions safe enough can order a so-called piano luxury case model. With the piano luxury case model, said my brother,

luxury piano case model, I interjected,

no, piano case luxury model, my brother insisted, with the piano luxury case model the outer case walls are made even more secure, fitted with 0.8 millimeters of strong sheet iron. Furthermore, if desired, so-called piano case rollers can be built into the inner walls of the piano case so that both during insertion—the rolling of the grand piano into the case before the beginning of transport—as well as during extraction—the rolling of the grand piano out of the case after the end of transport—the piano case rollers remove even the remotest possibility of damage being incurred during transport. But the most important condition that a case has to meet from the very beginning in order to be allowed to be called a case at all is that its walls must be at least an inch thick, which, however, they inexplicably are not in this case here, said my brother, finding fault with the Conservatory's case. On the inner piano transport case panel walls, of course, there should be inch-long strips of wood or metal at least every twenty centimeters, but preferably every fifteen or ten centimeters, strips that support the security latches on the corners of both the piano and the case. If such a mammoth case, piano case, is supposed to be used for tropical shipping, a so-called custom-made tropical piano transport case, I said,

no, a custom-made piano tropical transport case, my brother maintained,

a custom-made tropical transport piano case, I replied, but with the custom-made piano case tropical transport, explained my brother, it is absolutely essential that the inner walls of the case be lined with sheets of zinc. We are often called upon to make such cases when people emigrate to tropical regions. Or for concert tours through tropical regions, I said.

Correct, replied my brother, there are often pianists who have to undertake a concert tour through the hottest areas of our planet and who have become accustomed to traveling with and performing their concerts on their own grand pianos, and in recent times many pianists have become aware of the advantages of performing concerts with their own grand pianos, which practice has proven again and again to be of particularly great benefit for evening piano concerts in the tropical regions of our planet, because most of the pianos in the concert halls there have proven to be inferior, lacking in tonal quality.

On my concert tours, I replied, I often found, and not only in tropical countries, that there wasn't a poor or inferior piano in the concert halls, but rather no piano at all; in such cases I naturally turned immediately to the responsible concert organizer and asked for a piano, I absolutely needed a piano for the evening, after all, it was a so-called piano evening, but frequently the only answer I received was, what? a piano? why now suddenly a piano? they've never had a piano here, in all these years, no, in all these decades they've known how to get along perfectly well without a piano, and for the longest time the whole world also got along perfectly well without pianos, so why right now of all times do you need a piano, you see they didn't understand the need for one at all, and besides, lots of other pianists had already been there who got along fine without a piano.

It serves you right, said my brother, as a pianist you can avoid that sort of difficulty from the outset if you always travel with your own piano, the piano to which you are most accustomed, Ferruccio Busoni already understood the advantages of going on concert tours with his own piano. For that, the pianist needs a special case that's suited not only for transport into the extremely hot, but also into the extremely cold regions of the world, so that you can travel with it not only into the tropical but also into the polar areas of the planet; owing to its absolutely crack-free and airtight construction, guaranteeing maximum protection against the weather, this sort of packaging resists the harshest winter as well as the hottest summer, because in such a case the grand piano is packed not too differently from the way a preserved corpse is kept in a suitable casket. Also of great importance is the coating on the outer case walls, namely oil varnish, or else you stick to a pure varnish waterproofing of the wood. Whereas my competitors do not make their own piano transport cases, but rather use the ones provided by the piano manufacturers, I, in my business, said my brother, have succeeded in bringing about the innovation that I myself, the mover, personally have the piano transport cases constructed in my own case workshop, and I politely refuse the manufacturers' cases for the simple reason that I, as the mover, am responsible for trouble-free transport, and cannot, therefore, rely on cases provided by the manufacturers, but only on my own cases.

You should only trust your own cases, said my brother.

The cases made by the manufacturers were far inferior to the cases he manufactured in his own piano case workshop, where of course he could personally supervise and inspect the manufacturing of the piano cases. The cases made by the manufacturers are usually carelessly produced and designed, with visible flaws that are often apparent not only to the specialist but even to the layman. When, however, because of such a defective case from the piano manufacturers' workshops, an instrument is damaged in transport, it is not the piano manufacturer in question who is held responsible, who manufactured a poor case and basically should therefore be made responsible for the resulting damage, but rather the mover. So I can't make the piano manufacturer in question responsible in any way for his poor case. After it happened to my brother at the beginning of his career as a piano mover that several pianoforti were damaged during transport because of these inadequate piano manufacturers' transport cases, and he had both been held legally responsible and made to pay, he said to himself, no.

No, I said, said my brother, that's enough of the piano cases from the piano factories; granted, those people there know how to manufacture pianos to some extent, but in the construction of cases they're ridiculous dilettantes, I'll build my own cases myself, said my brother, and I won't let anyone interfere with any of my ideas about the cases. The people in the piano factories would do much better to restrict themselves to building their pianos, about which they know a fair amount, and they should give up manufacturing cases, about which they know absolutely nothing. Since then, my brother has built his own cases and, as he said, he has to this day been completely satisfied with his own cases. No one else's cases, absolutely no one else's cases, you always have the biggest problems with unfamiliar cases! Never again was a piano that was moved by my company damaged, not since the day when I began to work with my own cases! If the person who buys the piano doesn't insist on purchasing his case, the mover can use it more than once: a reusable case!

Then my brother crawled under one of the pianos to show me the path of the lower sounding board, which has a slightly bulbous upward inward curve, this slightly bulbous upward inward curve is absolutely essential for maintaining a perfect resonance effect, and when you air out a room that has a piano in it, my brother said, you should by no means close the piano while the room is being aired, but on the contrary open it to ensure an even distribution of the temperature fluctuations throughout the entire instrument at all times and to prevent a premature problem with the lower bulge of the sounding board, which problem will inevitably occur if this rule is repeatedly disregarded. It's complete nonsense to cover the piano! All the people who unnecessarily cover their pianoforti think they're doing their instruments a special service, but that's an error with far-reaching consequences, because only the upper covered parts of a piano are kept warm when you cover a pianoforte, while by contrast the lower, inward-curving sounding board remains cool, and a piano can't withstand such tension over time—on the one hand the lower inward-curving sounding board is cool, while on the other hand the upper covered parts of the instrument are more or less warm—keeping a piano covered causes a gradual disappearance of the bulge in the lower sounding board. Those leather coverings, too, that are custom-made in the leatherworks for the pianos in our conservatories and academies, those are complete nonsense, because they protect only the upper surface of the instruments, but not the lower pianoforte sounding board, and that's why most of the pianos in our conservatories and academies now have rickety sounding boards. But there are private owners too, explained my brother, who think, because they've seen that sort of thing in a conservatory or an academy, that they have to get a covering like that for their instruments at home too, because they naturally believe that the instruments in our conservatories are getting proper care. Every time I find out that a client is contemplating such machinations, I advise him most strongly not to do so. Your piano doesn't need leather clothing, I say to my clients again and again, you'd be better off buying yourself a leather coat for the wintertime, but not for your piano, I emphasize again and again. Nevertheless, an entire branch of the leather industry makes its living from the leather piano aprons that it makes not only for the conservatories and academies, but also for many private owners who have thus been led astray.

My brother knocked on the piano case with his tuning hammer, observing that it was a completely inadequate case, you see, a typical manufacturer's piano transport case, then he went into the piano case through the narrow opening, which was as tall as a man, and I was unable to refrain from closing it after him, he was locked in then and was crashing violently around, but I sat down at a nearby piano and struck a few chords, while my brother continued charging about in the case, quiet, I called to him, can't you hear that someone's making music out here, and if the two of us were locked into the attic, the brain of the music institute, then he was additionally, fittingly—as it seemed to me—now locked into a piano case, but unexpectedly the case opened sideways, it seemed an additional door had been built into the case that could be opened from the inside, something quite unusual, my brother walked out of the case, and we were both astonished by this otherwise uncustomary door.

Something entirely new, said my brother, a second door in the case, strange, he said, live and learn, and he thought about it with a strained expression. Soon, however, he had found the solution: placing the case at the disposal of the homeless, he called to me in a lively fashion, naturally, that's the solution!

See, he said, in the future we should always put a door there, so when the case is no longer useful for transport, we can give it away for philanthropic purposes!

Set them up around the city and put them at the disposal of the homeless! He took another look into the piano case, sizing it up.

There's room enough for a bed and a lamp in there, he said.

I'm going to suggest this to the district council first thing tomorrow! The city will be surrounded by inhabited piano cases!

New cities and villages of inhabited piano cases, shouted my brother.

Piano case cities, I thought, piano case villages. Entire landscapes full of piano cases.

Rent them, shouted my brother, do you hear me, rent them to people looking for apartments. When the piano cases aren't suitable for transporting pianos anymore, I can rent them to people looking for apartments, he explained, a business I could slowly build up and eventually hand over to you, what do you say to that?

Piano case landscapes, I thought.

You probably thought, he went on, you could lock me in there, let me freeze, you were mistaken, by the way, these days many people have started building heaters into their pianos, or having one built in at the factory, or, even better, having their instruments connected to the appropriate district heating plants, to keep them at the necessary even temperature at all times, of course they have to pay extra for that, and the civil servants at the district heating plants who do this off-site work not only have to receive prior training in heating technology, but also if possible know a little something about pianos, so that they know first of all how to connect not only a house or apartment, but also a piano to the district heating system, and second, so that they're able to assess at any given time whether an already connected piano was connected by a responsible district heating plant technician or improperly and "illicitly" by a district heating plant layman or even a district heating plant incompetent. The district heating plants guarantee the even heating of the entire piano sounding board, so that the lower bulge that curves upward always remains reassuringly constant. Unfortunately, the district heating plants have to this day neglected what should really be one of their primary duties, said my brother, which is to issue a public warning about the improper and harmful practice of covering pianos with leather, but the members of the board of directors of the leather industry to this day have always managed to defend themselves, in most cases the members of the board of directors of the district heating plants are in league with the members of the board of directors of the leather industry. Their training at the district heating plants still isn't as it should be, there's much too much district heating plant theory and far too little district heating plant practice, to be sure, but before entering the profession the civil servants do attend not only the district heating plant schools but also the music schools, conservatories, and academies, in order to have the necessary educational background for their profession, in fact a majority of the students at the conservatories and academies are the future civil servants of the district heating plants, and the sizeable crowd of people wanting to get positions at the district heating plants after they finish their studies at the academies and conservatories is significant! Still, most pianos are heated the wrong way! Through the skylights we heard a factory whistle presumably announcing the end of the working day. Do you hear the hissing of the district heating plant outside? asked my brother.

I was shaken then by an extremely violent withdrawal attack, the blood receded from my head, my hands, and my feet, my fingers closed to fists that I couldn't reopen, my entire body was rolled up, and then I fell over and couldn't move because everything in me was in an enormous cramp.

My brother got worked up and said: your organs, which are nothing more than mechanisms designed to assist your head—these, to use technical terminology, so-called auxiliary supports for your mind—are rebelling against the brain that is planning their destruction! Then he realized that our situation—being locked in—was at least potentially, temporarily desperate, and he tried to calm me down, wait, he said, just a minute, he took a hip-flask out of his jacket, unscrewed the lid, stuck the flask in my gasping mouth, and on the one hand not wanting it and on the other hand craving it I choked down the liquor, at first I had difficulty keeping the burning liquid down, but after draining his other, supplementary hip-flask I was almost back to normal again. In the near future, said my brother, as I stole the third hip-flask out of his jacket and finished it, you're going to have to go to detox anyway as soon as possible. Antabuse! my brother shouted at me, yes indeed, Anta-buse! I knew that every type of treatment would be completely in vain. I now found myself once again in one of those many cages of sound, caught between two imagined or actually struck notes, cages I wandered into again and again. Perhaps that's also the reason I can hardly compose anything anymore. I often refuse to let—or am incapable of letting—the next natural note follow upon a note I've struck or imagined, because I'm always waiting for something astonishing to happen between the two notes, just as I often get stuck in mid-sentence or mid-thought, never reach the next word, not even in my thoughts, though it may already be on the tip of my tongue, because I'm hoping for something unexpected to occur between these two words or partial thoughts; just as, when I force myself to think about what I want to write, it slips my memory again and again.

My brother turned back to the pianos once more, what a terrible tone, he shrieked, no wonder, someone mishandled a repair on the strong wooden crossbeam that runs over and behind the keyboard! And this on a conservatory piano, people are always having their pianos repaired not by experts but by roaming incompetents who take them in time and time again. Unfortunately it can't be helped that common piano laymen get taken in again and again by roaming incompetents, but to think that the incompetents are now sneaking into the conservatories! It's tragic that both the people who intended to learn tuning, repairing, polishing, etc., in the various piano factories and piano storerooms, but were incapable of learning these things, as well as the most motley collection of other characters, have turned to, of all things, the piano trade. Hairdressers, bakers, shoemakers, painters, wood-turners, civil servants, traveling salesmen, roofers, butchers and so on, who all want to improve their financial situations on the basis of new work as so-called "piano experts." Here! roared my brother and pointed angrily into a piano, these strings are strung too short! It's above all this infamous tying of strings that makes money for these incompetents! They tie thick strings between thin ones, long strings between short ones! Strings that have been thrown away, my brother roared. If you let an incompetent at your piano once, just once, you've not only thrown your money out the window, but your piano too. These incompetents often take off strings that have nothing wrong with them, say they have to be replaced, and then put the same strings back on again and bill you for it. In numerous cases these incompetents hawk their business around by getting together with pianists because they find jobs more easily when they get recommended by pianists, who in turn take a percentage from the incompetents. The pianists and the incompetents are in league! Throughout the world, pianos are being ruined by incompetents! A disastrous practice of theirs that is becoming more and more widespread is the so-called *higher tuning*, my brother explained. Often charlatan conductors will require a piano to be tuned higher by almost a whole tone over the normal *A*. Recently, when an expert refused to do this, the charlatan conductor had a incompetent come, who greedily took the job without hesitation. Shortly before he had finished the higher tuning, my brother explained, there was a terrible bang, because the piano, which could not withstand such tension, exploded, and several curious people who had been following the imbecile's work with great interest were mortally wounded! It happened in the middle of a marketplace, the evening before a fair, and all the people in the village ran down to the site together, thinking a bomb had gone off. Although the rescue crew arrived immediately, the curious people who had been completely unprepared for exploding pianos succumbed to their injuries immediately and couldn't be saved; they were killed, killed by flying piano splinters! And the incompetent, who was spared because he jumped aside at the last moment, was of course not held responsible. You have to know, explained my brother, that the tension created by a single piano string corresponds to a weight of at least seven hundred, but often a thousand kilograms, and the tension of all two hundred and thirty to two hundred and fifty strings strung in a piano must be equated to the weight of forty loaded freight cars!

So I told my brother that once in a conservatory a director had had not only all the pianos in all the rooms of his conservatory, but also those that were stored in the attic of the building, over a hundred instruments, simultaneously tuned higher by all the neighborhood incompetents, whereupon not only all the pianos but also all the conservatory rooms and the attic exploded simultaneously, the entire conservatory blew up in a flash and all the surrounding neighborhoods of the city in the area of the conservatory were buried in rubble.

That's strange, said my brother, I haven't heard that story before, but if people had used experts instead of incompetents, that sort of thing wouldn't have happened.

Even a blind tuner undergoes training for several years, and after finishing his music studies receives the so-called "blind tuner photo identification," my brother went on to explain. It's a proven fact that a blind person, who of course can't see anything, but can hear all the better for it, usually gives a piano a more well-tempered tuning than someone who still has his sight. Again and again, my brother explained, certain people try to obtain the advantages of the blind in this profession and pretend to be blind themselves. Therefore, when you're shown the blind tuner photo identification, you should be suspicious and check to see if it really is a blind person, even when he has a guide dog along you should know that this means nothing, because the dog could also be part of the disguise! And if the blind person shows up with an escort, you should make sure the piano is tuned by the blind person and not by the escort, because there are also tuners who see very well who always take along a blind person for appearance's sake.

From one of the attic windows I looked down on the city, where the houses had turned into large pianos the citizens were playing on, there were also a few lone harps standing between the trees, people shimmied up the strings as though they were climbing poles and then slid back down again, while several set sail, rocking on their instruments through the gray evening wind to the sea . . . my natural sensory organs, I thought, equip me for only the most superficial sensations and insights, because of the incompetence of my sensory organs I have to rely on banalities, from which my pitifully limited ability to take in stimuli does not allow me to escape, and even if I succeed at least temporarily in feigning to myself that I have surfaced from these banalities—by being able to survive reasonably unharmed despite breaking away from the so-called healthiness of nature, and, unfortunately, at least up until now, there's no other way I know how to get away from myself without burdening myself in new ways I can't hope to cope with—I'll soon be hauled in again and taken down by the so-called good sense that confines me all the more securely to the unimaginativeness that is the typical secretion of my narrow and limited sensory organs; perhaps, I thought, one day I will succeed in discovering a way to make myself capable of such sensations and perceptions so as to eclipse everything I've known up until now without also putting myself under such stress that I break down at the beginning of every extraordinary thing I experience, I thought to myself.

In the dusk, my brother and I tried to pass the time by playing piano duets on one of the terrible pianos, Schubert's "Storms of Life" and "Military Marches," in the meantime the sun had long since set outside, it was already almost entirely dark and we hadn't even noticed that the elevator motor had started, the elevator arrived, and a short fat man got out who, as we then saw, was wearing a gray work coat and shining an almost meter-long flashlight around, he turned on a light switch somewhere, whereupon a lightbulb hanging down from the roof truss began to light the room poorly, obviously it was the caretaker we'd been hoping would come, but instead of freeing us, he immediately began to scold us and accuse us in a disgraceful way, without letting my brother, who tried again and again to explain everything to him, get a word in edgewise.

You shut up right now, what could we have been thinking of, setting ourselves up here, making ourselves comfortable, probably for some time now, that sort of thing had never happened before, he wouldn't let us get away with it, he would take vigorous action, and the authorities would know how to deal with us, and quickly too, shady characters, tramps, probably wanted to steal something here, who possibly had already stolen something, and yes shut up, you have nothing to say, you're in no position to be vulgar and insolent, he was going to report everything right away to the Director, who would then turn us over to the police, that would have terrible consequences for us, and the pianos, the pianos were probably ruined now, how could we have had the audacity to touch the pianos, brand new instruments, a large portion of the valuable assets of the institute, naturally, and we'd opened them, we knew how to open the pianos, he'd seen it just now, whoever got too close to those instruments would really have to reckon with him, he usually wasn't like that, he usually kept his own council, he was basically too good-natured, but whoever did anything to the precious, irreplaceable instruments, he would really, then really, I told you to shut up. He discovered my brother's tuning hammer, took it from him, well what's this, and so on, but we couldn't fool him, no, it was a piano screwdriver, and now it was entirely clear what we were up to, but he had been able to prevent the worst of it, just in the nick of time, we were going to take the pianos apart, dismantle them, carry them away bit by bit under cover of darkness, have them disappear, that was just like us, we'd thought it out nicely but hadn't seen the whole picture, hadn't counted on his being there, and he had come just in the nick of time, and it was impossible to take apart even one piano behind his back, because he kept an eye on them at all times, and if we'd thought we could just fool around with his pianos, could be unscrewing them, unscrewing the pianos, then we were mistaken, he would have to report all this to the Director right away, the Director's eyes would pop out of his head, but you can't start shaking your head about everything outrageous that happens these days, you'd never finish shaking your head, but they couldn't let the sort of thing we were doing catch on, he had to put a stop to our game, to issue a warning, and he was going now to bring the Director up, he would be right back with the Director; no more excuses, roared the caretaker, there'll be no more excuses, we have all the evidence against you in our hands, here, the piano screwdriver, I'm taking it along, otherwise you'd make it disappear!

He got into the elevator and rode down. We stood there helplessly for a while; once again we had gotten into an unexpectedly unpleasant situation.

It's a good thing he's getting the Director, said my brother, he'll recognize us right away, and we'll explain everything to him.

It may not be the same Director anymore, I said, whom we knew in our student days.

It's out of the question, answered my brother, that there could have been a change of directors without my having heard about it. Only in the most terrible times of crisis does it happen that directors change or are exchanged yearly, or, in particularly extreme cases, monthly, so that you aren't always sure who the current director is.

There are often times, I replied, in which the directors are changed or exchanged with just such rapidity, and often the strangest people are appointed directors, so that it's quite possible that the caretaker, while fetching the director, will find out in the process that he himself, the caretaker, is the current director.

The elevator arrived, and the Director, who got out before the caretaker, was talking insistently to the caretaker, at first without paying any attention to us. Excellent to have informed him, the Director, right away, as soon as anything happens, report it to him immediately, that's what he's there for, so that people report everything to him immediately.

Always come right to me in every case when there's something going on, said the Director to the caretaker, so that I personally can take the matter in hand right away, and it's good that you came right away, and where are the burglars?

Suddenly, in the person of the Director, I recognized our old piano professor whom we had wanted to visit this afternoon, but hadn't found in his studio. And he recognized us as his former students, and on the one hand delighted and on the other hand astonished we greeted each other warmly.

We wanted to visit you this afternoon, explained my brother, it's a happy surprise for us, especially in this unpleasant situation, to find ourselves facing you, Professor Hellberger, and not the director we had expected.

It probably escaped your notice, Hellberger replied, but our previous director, of whom you speak, was handicapped by an unfortunate accident at work and found it necessary to take an early retirement, which we all regret very much, it's a great loss for all the members of the institute that Mr. Hofrat is no longer able to carry out his duties.

What's wrong with him, what happened? asked my brother.

That's not at all easy to explain, answered Hellberger, and no one really liked to dwell on it, it had been a piano lesson, the last piano lesson that Hofrat gave, Hofrat was teaching an exceptionally talented student, the student was playing a particularly quiet part of Prokofieff's "Toccata," I think, and in addition the student played this particularly quiet part particularly quietly, barely audibly, you know, so quietly in any case that the elderly director could hardly hear the quiet part that was being played so quietly; his hearing, Hellberger explained, wasn't what it used to be, if you must know, and in order to be better and more accurately able to assess the tonal and sound quality of this quiet part that his student was playing particularly quietly, Hofrat held his head, you know, like so. The professor demonstrated to us at one of the opened pianos how the elderly Hofrat must have held his head into the opening beneath the propped-up lid of the grand piano. See, like this, with his neck here on the outer edge, the Director's head explained from inside the piano, and his head, his ear here inside, over the strings, in order to be able to hear everything clearly, you know, and up above here, you see, exactly over his head, the propped-up lid; suddenly, then, the exceptionally talented student, immediately following the unusually quiet part, played an unbelievably loud part so loudly that the lid, you see, either because of the student's sudden loud playing, or because of an abrupt head movement by Hofrat, who was momentarily startled by the student's sudden loud playing, caused the stick here, you see, that props the lid up, to be jostled, so that the lid fell down instantly, right down on Hofrat's head, and so Hofrat's head was shut inside the grand piano and the rest of his body was outside the grand piano, and on this edge here, you see, the falling lid had almost cut off, severed Hofrat's head, which was inside the piano, cut it right through the neck, cut it from Hofrat's body, which was outside the grand piano, you know.

Now come and seat yourself at the piano! the professor ordered me.

I seated myself at the grand piano.

So, and now play a particularly quiet section of something, he ordered, as quietly as you can!

I played very quietly.

I'll put my head inside, said the professor. The professor stuck his head inside the grand piano again. And now suddenly play a particularly loud part, his head ordered me from inside the piano, and so abruptly I played particularly loudly.

And suddenly, Hellberger explained, as I jump, you see, I'm startled, the lid falls down, because as a result of this uncontrolled reflex movement I've moved the stick here with my neck, suddenly the lid falls down on my head, you see! The Director deliberately let the lid of the piano fall down toward his head on the inside of the piano, but at the last moment he pulled his head out, before the falling piano lid hit the edge of the piano with a terrible noise.

See, said the professor, it can happen that fast, this time it almost got me too. A severe displacement of the brain, Hellberger said to us then, you know, but above all the shock, so we suggested to Hofrat that he voluntarily take early retirement, a fine person, an uncommonly fine person. Then afterwards the government selected me and hired me to take over the direction of the institute, I've only recently had the honor of being responsible for the smooth running of all business in this building.

Then you are now the Director here, said my brother beaming with joy at the professor.

Yes, now I'm the Director here, answered Hellberger.

Well that's good, replied my brother, not only for you, but above all for the institute.

I'm glad to see you again after so many years, said Hellberger, we don't see each other nearly often enough and are always losing track of each other, don't you remember the two brothers anymore, he asked the caretaker, Fritz here is one of our most promising composers, and Otto here in the meantime has become the most respected piano mover in our city, you know, many years ago they were my favorite pupils and the most talented students, not only out of those who passed through my own studio, but in the entire Conservatory, it really wasn't necessary to intimidate the brothers, of all people, the way you told me you had, you got the two of them quite panicked!

Turning to us, Hellberger said, you shouldn't misunderstand the caretaker, he certainly didn't mean it like that, you know, during the war he was with the antiaircraft defense, and he still works in the reserves in his spare time, and that's quite something for someone his age, he's still the treasurer and deputy secretary for the Home Service, aren't you, said Hellberger to the caretaker who was nodding in agreement, it's good that you reported all this to me right away in person, you know, that's what I'm here for, so that I can take the matter in hand myself right away.

I'm glad to see you again after so many years, Hellberger said to us again, we don't see each other nearly often enough and are always losing track of each other, but to think that we're meeting again up here in the attic of the Conservatory, of all places, I find it, you know, strange.

That's exactly what I wanted to explain to the caretaker just now, replied my brother; and then there wouldn't have been any misunderstanding.

You must always let anyone you're dealing with explain everything in detail, said the Director to the caretaker, listen carefully when someone is speaking to you, let the person finish and don't interrupt him, I've noticed that you sometimes try to mimic me, you try to imitate me, and always, when you think I'm not watching, you mimic me, you were probably trying to mimic me again just now when you were up here alone with the brothers, weren't you? you were mimicking me then, am I right? of course you were mimicking me, well?

The caretaker stood there silently and motionless. There's no harm in admitting that you were trying to mimic me just now up here, said the Director to the caretaker, I'm certainly not angry with you about it! Well?

The caretaker nodded.

Well see, said the Director, I knew it, you were trying to mimic me again; is that really necessary?

Then my brother recounted everything that had happened very precisely, that we had wanted to visit Hellberger this afternoon, how we were suddenly standing outside the Conservatory, that at first I couldn't be persuaded to go into the Conservatory because I was afraid that after so many years we'd get lost in the building and wouldn't find the right studio, how he, my brother, then persuaded me to at least try to enter the building to pay a visit to him again, Professor Hellberger. And then we had found the right studio right away, my brother told the professor, without much searching around at all, as though we had last been there only yesterday, we found it in the shortest time imaginable, and suddenly we were standing in front of your studio door, Director, just imagine, said my brother.

Congratulations, said Hellberger, but of course you only succeeded in finding it because I have always taught in the same room, have taught there for decades now, ever since I became a member of the institute, quite unlike my colleagues, who are always changing or exchanging their studios: several times a week, in extreme cases, but at least once a semester. I hate this constant exchanging of studios, and in this regard I do *not* understand my colleagues at all, and as far as I'm concerned, I'm not one of those studio changers, no, I'm no studio changer, let alone one of those regular studio exchangers, but rather am still teaching today—insofar as my new main job as Director of the institute will permit me—in the same studio. Of course after the government entrusted me with the direction of the institute I immediately tried to put an end to both this constant exchanging of studios as well as the constant changing of studios by announcing the strictest bans on changing and exchanging studios. But now my colleagues simply change and exchange their studios behind my back, without my being able to prevent it, and indeed with such speed that in many cases I, the Director, am incapable of noticing that it's going on at all. Unfortunately, I am powerless against such outrages, because as Director I have such a diverse number of responsibilities to manage that I am unfortunately not in a position to concern myself with such problems intensively and extensively enough, or to give them the necessary care that would be required in order for me to be able to take vigorous action and achieve any degree of success. The unaccustomed responsibility that rests on one as Director! said the Director, this afternoon for example I was on my way to a particularly urgent conference, which is probably why you didn't, unfortunately, find me in.

No, we didn't find you in and were very sad, said my brother, my dear Director, and wanted to leave the Conservatory right away again, but in the corridor quite unexpectedly we happened to see the open elevator door, and quite spontaneously, almost without noticing, we got in and rode up to the attic.

Now he understood everything, said Hellberger, now everything was clear to him, both in order to summon the elevator from outside as well as to open the outer elevator door you needed a so-called *lift key*, which of course we didn't have at our disposal. Once you're in the elevator, you don't need a lift key anymore to set the elevator in motion, you just need to press the respective button, then it starts to move, the elevator, but to summon it and be able to open it, you need the lift key.

The open elevator door was your misfortune, said the professor, you should never have entered the elevator nor set it in motion, you know, then you would have been spared all this.

You always have to close the elevator door properly, do you understand? said Hellberger then to the caretaker. You can't just go around leaving the elevator door open, what are you thinking of? Always close the elevator carefully, Hellberger roared at the caretaker, not like this afternoon, when you forgot to close the elevator before you left it, even if it was just for a short time, because that's the only way it could have happened that the brothers rode up here in the elevator! Actually, you're to blame for everything, because if you had always, including today, closed the elevator carefully, as required by the regulations, even when you were only away from it for a short period of time, the brothers would have been spared all this! Don't let this happen again, in future you must guard the elevator even more closely than before, so that no more unauthorized people get in.

We understand each other, don't we!

Yes, they understood each other, the caretaker nodded.

And as you know anyway, said Hellberger to the caretaker, pupils and students are expressly forbidden to use the elevator, the pupils must without exception go on foot and take the stairs! Turning to us again, Hellberger explained, unfortunately, without the lift key you had no other way of getting down from the attic, because the part of the stairwell that used to link the attic with the lower stories was destroyed in the last war. Then he said to the caretaker, everything's all right now, you ride down first, I'll come later with the brothers, you should go to bed, I'm sure you're already tired, it's gotten late, and remember to check carefully that all the entrances of the Conservatory are properly locked, so that no unauthorized person can get into the Conservatory at night! The caretaker disappeared with the elevator.

With renewed pleasure at seeing us again, a pleasure that now, after the caretaker had left us alone, was able to become somewhat more intimate, Hellberger said he was certainly glad to see us again after so many years, we don't see each other nearly often enough and are always losing track of each other, and he asked how we were, we should tell him, and turning to me he said, congratulations on the premiere of your Five Big Pieces for Orchestra, opus 5, naturally I've followed your career, the premiere was in Stockholm, I think, oh no, excuse me, in Amsterdam, of course, and with the excellent Concertgebouw Orchestra, no less, whose old chief conductor, Willem Mengelberg, who has unfortunately been dead now for so many years, I had the honor to meet personally, if only briefly, at a banquet, you know, at a reception held by our prime minister at the time to honor the members of the orchestra on the occasion of their only concert here, as you see, I'm right up to date on you and your work, do tell me, he said to my brother, are you very busy with your moving business, you move pianos everywhere in the world, don't you? that's really something, and turning again to the two of us together he asked how our mother was, whom he had not had the honor of seeing again in a very long time, as you know, I've always been extraordinarily fond of your mother and have always tried to show her particular respect, the two of you will certainly still remember the many Saturday and Sunday afternoons we spent together, either at your country house or in one of our Conservatory rooms, and your mother, though she hardly had time to practice, proved also to be a splendid pianist and is certainly still a splendid pianist today, how we practiced and played the Bach concertos for three and four pianos together, and sometimes Kurt Wenzel joined in our weekend music *privatissime* as well, the two of you will still remember him, he played the orchestra parts on a fifth piano.

Oh yes, my brother replied, Wenzel, of course, how is he, Kurt, what's he up to?

Wenzel's fine, answered Hellberger, things are going really well for him, because today—and that's really something for someone his age—he's the head attorney with the district medical insurance company. In his spare time he conducts the so-called Employees' Spare Time Chamber Orchestra. The members of the Employees' Spare Time Chamber Orchestra meet not only every Friday evening right after the week's work and then spend the weekend days and nights making music under Wenzel's direction, right through until Monday morning when the next work week begins, but also every Monday Tuesday Wednesday and Thursday evening right after work, they spend the rest of the evenings and nights making music right through until morning when they have to go back to work again. In this manner Wenzel has taught his people remarkable musical discipline. Once a year all the members of the orchestra go on the popular Employees' Spare Time Chamber Orchestra outing, in the course of which they put on a first-class chamber music concert in the church or the conference hall of the town they've gone to on their outing, with the greatest success, to lively applause from a large audience of locals.

While Hellberger was talking, my withdrawal symptoms made themselves felt again, above all a strong urge to throw up, which I couldn't conceal from the Director.

What's with him? he asked my brother, what's wrong with your brother?

That's difficult to say, answered my brother and whispered in the Director's ear: We can trust you, can't we, Director, we can count on you to be discreet?

Of course we could trust him, answered the Director with a smile, what were we thinking of, who else should we trust, you probably don't know that I was also a close friend of your father's when he was alive, the two of you didn't really have the opportunity to get to know him well because as you've probably been told he was unfortunately killed in the Second World War, blown up by a flat antitank mine in the Sahara Desert!

My pains increased. What's wrong with your brother? the Director asked my brother.

It's difficult to explain, said my brother, but since we could rely on him, the Director, to be discreet, you know, to tell you the truth, bluntly, my brother is a heavy binge drinker, right now he's getting over one of his binges, hence the withdrawal pains we're seeing, they'll pass, in a few days he'll feel normal again, my brother explained to the Director, when the withdrawal pains have disappeared, at least until the next binge.

Then the rumors going around about your brother are true, replied the Director, at first I didn't want to believe it, but unfortunately I kept hearing things.

Do talk with him, Director, said my brother, he doesn't listen to me, maybe he'll listen to you, just now I offered him a position in the piano moving business again to tear him away from his always sitting around and moping so unproductively. Just think, said my brother to the Director, for years now he's hardly composed anything and has completely neglected his piano playing!

What, roared the Director, neglected his piano playing! Now I know what's been bothering me about you, what I've been noticing about you since I first came in! Don't you notice anything? he asked my brother.

I was sitting exhausted at one of the pianos, doubled over by my withdrawal attack.

His posture at the piano, roared the Director to my brother before he turned to me.

Haven't I preached to you a hundred times, he roared, that a stooping posture of the upper body at the piano is intolerable? But you're sitting there like a beginner with a hunchback! That probably comes from sitting much too low at your own piano!

You'll have to make sure to get your brother higher seating in future! he explained to my brother.

The Director straightened the chair I was sitting on and pushed my body into a proper piano-playing posture.

You should avoid wearing uncomfortable clothing when playing the piano too, he said, I see the pants you're wearing are far too tight! You have to wear loose pants if you want to play the piano properly, explained the Director, very loose and wide pants!

You'll have to make sure, he explained to my brother, that your brother wears wider pants in future, when he's playing the piano.

So, and now play a piano piece that you think you know reasonably well. I started playing one of Schoenberg's pieces, very quietly, the Director pulled a metronome out of his jacket, set it up and let it run, then he put his head into the opened piano, just as he had earlier when describing his predecessor's accident, he pulled his head out again immediately, though, right before I suddenly played the very loud part that followed the very quiet part in that piece. He's probably afraid the lid will fall down on his head, I thought.

Stop, he said, stop, stop right now, what are these impossible movements you're making while playing the piano, you've picked up some bad habits and are making all sorts of wrong movements, I had probably been neglecting to practice regularly with the mirror, he said, you know you absolutely have to practice with the mirror every day, wait, there's a piano mirror up here, see. He pushed out a tall standing mirror mounted on wheels and brought it into position beside me at the piano so that I could observe every one of my movements while playing. I noticed that the Director was keeping his left hand in his pants pocket and only bringing it out when it was absolutely necessary, after which he let it disappear right back into his pocket again. It's so you don't lose control of your movements while playing the piano, but observe yourself constantly, explained the Director, most people fail, not just as pianists, because at the wrong time they make precisely the wrong movement, or they make the wrong movement at precisely the wrong time, added my brother, quite right, replied the Director, and in order to make sure that sort of thing doesn't happen we use the piano mirror from time to time. Please make sure your brother starts practicing regularly with the mirror again, the Director said to my brother, asking did we even have a piano mirror at home, otherwise he could lend us this one for a while, also I should never play without a metronome, and he asked whether we had a functioning metronome at home, otherwise I can lend you this one here, you know, he said.

Keep playing, he called to me, and I kept playing, he let the metronome keep ticking and urged me again and again to look in the piano mirror.

No, no, he interrupted me, shaking his head, the best thing for you would be to start all over again at the beginning, Zuschneid, *Piano Method*, Volumes 1 and 2, and Czerny, *Schule der Geläufigkeit*.

Does your brother, he asked my brother, have the opportunity at home to practice undisturbed, at any time, for as long as he wants?

Yes, my brother replied, and in accordance with my wishes he had even set up a comfortable studio for me in the attic of our house. My brother described to the Director the size and arrangement of my attic studio, particularly the studio window, where a section of the roof had been replaced by glass bricks so that the light came in from above unobstructed, through an enormous glass surface, rather than just a tiny window. In this attic studio, that could be heated in the winter and cooled by an air-conditioner in the summer, as my brother explained to the Director, I had only ever been disturbed once, as far as my brother knew, and that was by a roofer who'd fallen off the roof while he'd been making urgently needed repairs.

Then my brother described this incident to the Director precisely, I remembered my brother had been standing in the courtyard of our house watching the roofer doing the repairs. Suddenly he noticed, my brother told the Director, that the roofer wasn't wearing a safety harness.

I remembered my brother calling up to the roofer on the roof, listen, you aren't wearing a safety harness, isn't that dangerous, or something like that, whereupon I heard the worker shout back down, what, he didn't understand, and he asked my brother if he would please talk a little louder, whereupon my brother called up to the worker again, listen, you're climbing around up there without a safety harness, or something like that, and what if you suddenly fell down, whereupon the worker, roaring with laughter, shouted back down that he had never fallen off a roof in his entire life, ridiculous, wearing a safety harness, after all he had learned, and he spoke, I think, of roof movement specialist courses he had taken, to be able to move around freely and safely on any roof without falling down right away, and besides, the masters, the real leaders in the field of roofing just didn't bother with safety harnesses, they're awkward, a waste of working time, etc.

Didn't he maybe want to use a safety harness anyway, I shouted back up, my brother told the Director, and hadn't the union recently issued a ruling that roofers should all use safety harnesses, he, my brother, had added. Leave me alone, the roofer called back impudently, just imagine, Director, my brother said, but while he was impudently shouting leave me alone, he suddenly slipped on the tiles, slid backwards while still shouting impudently, Director, the roofer slid along the sloped roof, at first slowly, then faster and faster, scraping right down over the glass bricks of the studio window, which of course he couldn't cling to, they accelerated his downward slide, Director, and having reached a high velocity, Director, the roofer reached the edge of the roof and fell off, screaming loudly.

While my brother was describing this, I could naturally see it happen all over again, I remembered how suddenly I had heard a scraping, then a rattling, then a crashing and a banging that got louder and louder, naturally I wondered how there could suddenly be this scratching and drumming of hail on the roof when we had sunshine and a clear blue sky, but then I already saw the blurred, indistinct outline of the roofer's body like the shadow of a bird over the glass roof gliding diagonally down directly over me, and then I heard his terrible scream of despair.

My brother went on to describe to the Director how he had still wanted to tell the fallen roofer, who had already landed with a smack and was then lying motionless there before him, see, if only you'd been wearing a safety harness all that wouldn't have happened to you, and my brother was so surprised by it all that it was only when he felt the urge to continue reprimanding the roofer that he became aware all at once that of course the man must have been killed on the spot.

It's deplorable that there's no relying on workers these days, replied the Director, I hope you drew the necessary conclusions from this incident and transferred your roof repairs to another roofing company at once.

Of course, my brother replied, we immediately cancelled the contract with that first firm, because a roofing business whose roofers are always falling down just can't be trusted.

Unfortunately, I had been sitting in my attic studio just then and had seen the roofer whiz down the glass roof over me, my brother said.

My brother is right, I've refused to go into my studio since then.

Above all I just couldn't move around as naturally as before in the light that fell into my studio through the same glass bricks on which the roofer's deadly fall had become unstoppable.

Neither my brother nor the Director showed the least understanding for my feelings on this point, Hellberger barked at me gruffly: you should be locked in your attic and not let out anymore, just like these pianos here, just like them, yes sir, listen, these pianos can't be allowed down from the attic ever again, you heard me correctly, said the Director to us, and turning to my brother he said, just as you can rely on me to be discreet about your brother's alcoholism, I trust I can rely on you to be discreet about this attic and the pianos here. Above all you mustn't tell anyone, I repeat, not anyone anything about these pianos being kept here, and in order to be able to explain this request to you, I've sent the caretaker down ahead of us, to this day he doesn't understand the far-reaching implications of the story. You two are the first and only outsiders who've been to the Conservatory attic in many decades, said Hellberger, an unfortunate coincidence, and other than my predecessors in this office, most of whom are already dead, myself, a few people I trust implicitly, and now also the two of you, no one knows about all these terrible pianos, by the way there are exactly 111 of them, and if the public were to get even an inkling that they were here, which is what all of us fear very much, then we might as well close the Conservatory. These pianos were donated to the Conservatory many decades ago, a few years before the beginning of the First World War, by a patron who didn't wish to be named, you heard correctly, donated to us. It's said that one day back then 111 horse-drawn carts pulled up to the Conservatory and took their places around the building; presumably the people inside were a little worried at first, because when a building is suddenly surrounded by 111 horse-drawn carts, well, this is usually not a very good sign. But then, as the story goes, one of the coachmen went into the Conservatory and handed the Director a letter to the following effect: Dear Director, as I hear it, the intellectual and particularly the musical education of the populace is not what it could be; I would like to make a contribution to the rectification of this imbalance in what seems to me the most suitable manner, and thus am herewith donating to your Institute 111 pianoforti—presumably the patron chose the number 111 as a reminder of the opus number of Beethoven's last piano sonata. The Director at that time, said the Director, an uncommonly fine person, was very pleased with the new pianos, but he immediately did the only correct and reasonable thing that can be done in such a situation: he had the instruments stored up in the Conservatory attic right away, you see the attic at the time was not only perfectly suited for the storing of instruments, but had even been planned with that in mind, and the pianos had above all to be preserved for posterity, since you don't put brand new pianos in the studios when the old instruments are still usable, no, you wait, and when the old instruments break, you fall back on your store of new pianos, or so the Director at the time must have thought, the Director explained to us. Years went by, and then unfortunately the First World War broke out, as you perhaps know. During the First World War, the Conservatory building was largely spared, only the roof was slightly damaged, but the storage conditions for the pianos, which had already been almost forgotten, were no longer ideal. The instruments should have been transferred right away to a proper storage facility, explained the Director, but in the difficult post-war period the Conservatory simply didn't have the financial wherewithal to repair the damage to the roof, nor to rent a suitable storage hall. During the Second World War, which followed soon afterwards, our building was again largely spared, except that a bomb hit in the vicinity of the Conservatory, and this—plus the concussion wave that followed—made the damage to the roof even worse. Still, after the Second World War, the Director explained, the instruments could have been saved by transferring them to a proper storage facility, and by undertaking some urgently needed but relatively minor repairs, which nevertheless were only postponed again and again because no one could agree on who was to take up the job. In the meantime, deliberations continued as to whether the pianos should be set up in the studios, distributed evenly in the classrooms, mostly because, as time went on, the horrendous weight of over one-hundred pianoforti in the attic would put enormous strain on the upper stories of the building and then finally on the whole Conservatory. At last they calculated that the cost of all the necessary repairs would substantially exceed the cost of buying perhaps not quite so many but almost as many new pianos; and then, taken in by an astoundingly low estimate for repair costs, they let a complete incompetent make a terrible mess of the inside of the instruments, as you've seen, said the Director, and that's how we came to have 111 valuable but completely unusable, brand-new pianos in the attic of the Conservatory, which no one has ever really played, and which above all no one will ever really be able to play, said the Director, and since the public can't be allowed to find out anything about the condition of these pianos, the very existence of the instruments has been covered up, kept from the populace, and I'm counting on you to be absolutely discreet, emphasized the Director. He said: Our thoughts are continually occupied with how we can make these instruments, which, although brand new, are nevertheless useless, disappear without anyone noticing, it's not easy to have 111 pianos simply disappear, you know, just loading them onto trucks in the dark of the night would immediately attract all those journalists who always roam the city at night, they'd come out of their hiding places and in no time at all everything would be known, the good name of the Institute would be ruined, we would have no option but to close down; we went so far as to make the instruments inaccessible to unauthorized people, we even had the staircase to the attic, which the two of you will certainly have sought several times in vain, removed!

The Director said: *Our thoughts are ruled by the unusable instruments that we have to keep secret!*

Chop them up and burn them, I said immediately, chop them up and burn them, said my brother too, my brother's right, said my brother, chop them up and burn them, that's the solution, Director, first you have the pianos chopped up, you know, then burned, and then, well, then you gradually have new pianos brought up here that I can obtain for you at a good price with my connections.

How could we get away with that? the Director said, chopping them up, the noise of chopping up the pianos, the sounds of chopping wood, for weeks, everyone passing by would be able to hear it, the people would think the Conservatory was mainly an Institute for Chopping Wood! And burning them, said the Director, where, just tell me where, because not only the Conservatory but also almost all the other buildings around here are connected to the various district heating plants, which do all our heating for us. For miles and miles around there aren't any proper stoves in which the pianos could be burned—or can you tell me where there's even a single stove nearby? no? well, there you have it.

Chop them up and give them to a district heating plant to burn, I said to the Director, you can't begin to imagine how much fuel is burned in a district heating plant.

It wouldn't work, answered the Director, not so much because of the district heating plant as because of the chopping.

But while the Director continued to talk to us about the pianos, the instruments began to play on their own: without anyone touching the keyboards, the rusted strings sounded through the worm-eaten wood on their undersides, and then they hopped through the attic and tried to jump out into the night, and then there were figures sitting at the pianoforti who put on a memorable concert, playing not only notes but sentences, incomprehensible words that were whispered and called aloud, directed at me, they swore at me in chorus, closed in on me, mounted me really, then one of the pianos tried to swallow me, pushing a thick, limp, brown block of wood ahead of it that thankfully swung back into the jaws of the instrument whenever I threatened it, a pink vapor was rising up from between the rows of keyboard teeth, and now something quite furry was present as well, yes, hair was growing on the instruments, hair that shone colorfully through the attic twilight, and then they began having sex with each other, mating in wild confusion, kicking up a lot of dust, moaning and creaking around the room, sweating, swinging over each other, and if only Hellberger had seen that . . .

We live with and in the constant fear, but also the certainty, said Hellberger, that some day, inevitably, everything will become known, and we'll have to close the Conservatory, whose good reputation will then be ruined, because no one could possibly set any store on attending such a conservatory, yes, someday we'll have to close the Conservatory.

So, he said then, now we want to go back downstairs at last, you two have been up here long enough I'm sure and will be happy to get away at last. We could still drink a little schnapps or a glass of wine at my place, in the office, you know, or in my studio . . . we haven't seen each other in such a long time, we don't see each other nearly often enough and are always losing track of each other, let's have a little schnapps in the office, but you, you get apple juice!

As you now know, you need a so-called lift key to bring the elevator up and to open the elevator door, if only you'd known that this afternoon, when you went into the open elevator.

With his right hand he took a large ring of keys out of his pants pocket. Oh no, he exclaimed then, don't tell me I have the wrong key ring with me, yes sir, the wrong key ring, just imagine, but if I'm not mistaken there's a lift key on this key ring too. As you can imagine, here in the Conservatory—for reasons you're now more than adequately familiar with—the elevator is the only possible way up to the attic, and we have to be careful and cautious with the lift keys to prevent one of them from getting into the wrong hands.

What bad luck, gentlemen, unfortunately there's no lift key on this key ring, just think, I need two key rings, you know, but can only have one key ring with me at a time, the two key rings together would be too heavy and wouldn't fit into my pocket, in this pocket there's only room for one key ring, and just this one key ring has my pocket bulging right out, see?

He drummed on the elevator door with his fists and called the caretaker.

Now I know what you're thinking, he said, of course I know, just put your second key ring in the other pocket, that's what you're thinking, you were going to say that to me, weren't you? But in my left pocket I always have, well, what do you think, correct, my hand, see, my hand is always in my left pocket, and I don't see why I shouldn't allow my left hand the left pants pocket. I simply need two key rings, he said, as the Director of such a large Institute I can't get along with just one key ring.

The light went out, it was completely dark, and a substantial amount of rain from an arriving low-pressure system began to drum on the roof.

Patience, gentlemen, said Hellberger, don't worry; Mr. Mairitsch will be here right away, or else Mr. Edelmann.

Again he drummed his fists on the elevator door and shouted down.

You know, he explained, we have two caretakers in the building, Mr. Mairitsch and Mr. Edelmann, we could never get along with only one caretaker in the Institute, and he drummed again on the elevator door and shouted Mr. Mairitsch, Mr. Edelmann.

But getting back to business, Otto, so that we understand each other, he said then to my brother, of course I will ensure in future that all official piano moving contracts go to you and your firm alone, the deal of your life, you can take my word on that, however, in return I really do want to be able to rely on you to keep quiet about what you've seen, heard, and experienced up here today. If you don't abide by this promise, I will unfortunately be forced to find suitable ways and means to drive all your clients away from you and your firm, to have next to all official and private contracts withdrawn, so that you'd have to close your business, we understand each other, don't we? Of course we understand each other, answered my brother.

And as far as your brother is concerned, said the Director, and of course I couldn't see in the darkness, but I felt him pointing at me, it would be better for him too if he held his tongue, but if he goes ahead and talks anyway, then by all means let him talk as much as he wants, your brother is a completely unimportant individual, no one takes him seriously anymore, and even my natural discretion about his alcoholism couldn't possibly improve people's opinions of him at this point, not only your brother's reputation but also he himself is, as you can see, as good as ruined.

It got light again, the elevator arrived, the caretaker got out.

Finally, Mr. Mairitsch, said the Director, where were you, did something happen?

A short circuit, answered the caretaker, a short circuit, Director, just imagine, suddenly it was dark everywhere, I woke Mr. Edelmann immediately, who was already sleeping and hadn't noticed anything at all, because I don't know a lot about electricity, but Mr. Edelmann got up right away and repaired the short circuit in no time, now it's light again everywhere, Director, isn't it, but you weren't here this afternoon, I forgot to give you an important message from your secretary: The senior building-code official has requested prompt action on the refurbishment of our sanitation facilities, the board of directors of the district heating plant wishes to inform you that after next week the Conservatory can only be heated at half the energy, and the minister called, he wants to arrange a meeting for the afternoon of the day after tomorrow or the morning of the day after the day after tomorrow to discuss the demolition and reconstruction of the Conservatory.

And while we rode down in the elevator, the caretaker said to the Director: One other thing, Director, a man called, he's sending the Conservatory a number of new pianos at no cost, it's supposed to be over a hundred of them. The man said he'll have the instruments delivered sometime next week.

In the Conservatory lavatory strange flowers and plants were growing out of the urinal shells, sometimes there were also varicolored, differently patterned bird feathers, it seemed to me as though I was in a botanical-zoological hothouse, and carnivorous lianas were steaming in through the window.

The people who met us on the street were wearing burning hats, and the ones who weren't wearing hats had their burning hair fluttering in the wind. The fire on the heads floating past them didn't bother the people at all because it was confined to their heads without extending to their bodies, yes, only their hat or their hair was ablaze, without really speading. Be careful that we don't collide with all these burning people and catch on fire, I said to my brother, who didn't answer me at all, because he was incapable of seeing these people, yes, my own head had made itself independent of me again without my being able to stop it, it was a balloon long since torn away from the falling gondola beneath it, carried away far out over the open sea, and from all the trees and bushes the leaves whispered to me that *the hair of the sky is the skin of the river the dress of the ocean is saltier than the sweat of the people*, etc., then the last thing I saw was the continents and other islands in the oceans and the seas connected with them being boiled thoroughly until a thick murky liquid was produced that was notable for its particularly persistent glue-like stickiness,

for a long time now I've barely been able to feel that I was a person at all, but instead only a (more or less miserable) condition *that was being communicated to me via my head—that instrument for measuring conditions—and this is presumably the reason why, from the time I first strayed into this city, without initially realizing what I was up to, and utilizing a system that has ever since been endlessly, gradually, geometrically disintegrating, I have up till this point in my life been so methodically and so eloquently destroying that very head.*